Karin Slaughter grew up in a small south Georgia town and has been writing short stories and novels since she was a child. She is the author of the Grant County series of international bestsellers *Blindsighted, Kisscut, A Faint Cold Fear, Indelible, Faithless* and *Skin Privilege*, and the bestselling thrillers set in Atlanta, *Triptych* and *Fractured*. She is also the editor of *Like A Charm*, a collaboration of British and American crime fiction writers. She lives in Atlanta.

Praise for Karin Slaughter

'Without doubt an accomplished, compelling and complex tale, with page-turning power aplenty' *Daily Express*

'No one does American small-town evil more chillingly . . . Slaughter tells a dark story that grips and doesn't let go' *The Times*

'A great read . . . crime fiction at its finest' MICHAEL CONNELLY

'Slaughter deftly turns all assumptions on their head . . . Her ability to make you buy into one reality, then another, means that the surprises – and the violent scenes – keep coming' *Time Out*

'A fast-paced and unsettling story . . . A compelling and fluid read' *Daily Telegraph*

'Criminally spectacular' *OK!*

Also by Karin Slaughter

Blindsighted
Kisscut
A Faint Cold Fear
Indelible
Faithless
Triptych
Skin Privilege
Fractured

Like a Charm (Ed.)

Karin Slaughter

martin misunderstood

arrow books

Published by Arrow Books 2008

2 4 6 8 10 9 7 5 3 1

Copyright © Karin Slaughter 2008

First published in Great Britain in 2008 by
Century
Random House, 20 Vauxhall Bridge Road,
London SW1V 2SA

www.rbooks.co.uk

Addresses for companies within The Random House Group Limited can be
found at: www.randomhouse.co.uk/offices.htm

The Random House Group Limited Reg. No. 954009

A CIP catalogue record for this book
is available from the British Library

ISBN 9780099525899

The Random House Group Limited supports The Forest Stewardship
Council (FSC), the leading international forest certification organisation.
All our titles that are printed on Greenpeace approved FSC certified paper
carry the FSC logo. Our paper procurement policy can be found at
www.rbooks.co.uk/environment

Typeset by SX Composing DTP, Rayleigh, Essex
Printed and bound in Great Britain by CPI Bookmarque Ltd,
Croydon, CR0 4TD

To Georgina, the unsung hero

Martin Explained, or How Martin Unwittingly Became a Person of Interest

Martin Reed had decided long ago that he was born into the wrong body. He often wondered how different his fate would have been if that amorphous lump that stared vacantly from his first photograph at the hospital had shown even the slightest bit of potential. But, no, it was clearly not meant to be. The picture of baby Martin, thrusting himself into the air like a bloated seal, wet, pink lips parted, chin sliding into his neck even then, and – perhaps worst of all – the words 'Mama's Little Angel' emblazoned over his grayish, hairless head, would be one that would haunt him throughout his entire life.

It wasn't that Martin was a dreamer. He did not think, for instance, that George Clooney had gotten his true face. Nor did he see Brad Pitt's physique and spit bitter 'if only' vitriol. He would have been fine with an average man's body, something his many hours on his Chuck Norris Total Gym system could exploit into the semblance of muscle tone instead of a lateral realignment of flab. Even Will Ferrell's physique would have sufficed. The cruel truth of the matter was that Martin's body more closely resembled Jodie Foster's during her Yale years. Add in his weak chin, his hawkish nose and the C-shaped curve to his shoulders, and the root of his displeasure (and that of many blind dates) became painfully apparent.

His life was just the sort of pathetic life you would expect of Jodie Foster's estranged, less attractive fraternal twin. Working as a senior accountant at Southern Toilet Supply for the last sixteen years, he had become somewhat resigned to the small-town Georgia life into which he had been born. The bullies with whom he had attended high school had become the jerks with whom he worked. The cheerleading captain who had spurned his attention continued to do so, but this time from behind a desk instead of behind pom-poms. Norton Shaw, his Geometry Team nemesis, had been promoted to his direct supervisor. Even the security guard was the same man who had walked the halls of Tucker High School; he had been fired for stalking one of the cafeteria ladies, a crime which, apparently, did not bother the denizens of Southern Toilet Supply.

Upon reflection, Martin's life was typical in that it had not changed much after leaving high school. But then for Martin, life seldom proved atypical. Striving for normalcy had been his elusive life goal. He was of average height, average intelligence, average weight – so why was it that he came across as so blatantly below average? Fortunately, he had other things to recommend himself: A steady job. A Toyota Camry that was almost paid for. An intricate knowledge of the toilet-supply industry.

It must be said that, for most of his life, Martin had tried to make changes. A lifelong reader, he had at first turned to books for help. He had read *Chicken Soup* for every type of soul. *The Power of Positive Thinking* had left him thoroughly depressed. To his horror, he'd discovered that he shared more characteristics with people from Venus than from Mars. *The Secret* had arrived around the time that a series of disasters befell him: pinkeye, an incident on a faulty escalator, 'twat' being keyed into his car. Martin had cuddled up with the book, a warm washcloth over one eye, and soon discovered that it was entirely his own fault.

Martin's mother was equally dissatisfied with her son – perhaps more so. Often, she would look at him over the breakfast table (of course he still lived with his mother) and make grand pronouncements about his shortcomings.

'Goodness, I think you lost more hair last night.'

'My, you should see how that roll of fat hangs over your belt.'

'You know, there are women you can pay for companionship.'

Evelyn Reed, on first glance, was the quintessential sweet old lady. Until she opened her mouth. Like Martin, she was an outsider, the sort of person who did not easily make friends. Unlike Martin, she assumed the blame lay with others and was not a direct result of her abhorrent personality. Most days, he thought of her as some awful troll who refused to allow him to cross the bridge into a new, more exciting life. Other days, he felt more generous and only saw her as an old woman who, hopefully, would soon die so that he could lead a new, more exciting life.

Many of the recurrent dreams in Martin's head ended happily with his mother passing on to some great ether. As he chewed his turkey bacon or drank his prune juice, Martin would imagine himself a character in a book; some kind of broad comedy with murderous undertones. *Case Histories*, but without the happy ending. His words would be in quotation marks. His thoughts in italics.

'Mother, can you pass the butter knife?' *Would you please jam it into your chest first?*

Evie Reed had been an attractive woman at some point in her life, a point which, surprisingly, had gone wholly undocumented. There were no pictures that captured this great beauty, no witnesses to back up her statements. It strained credulity to see her now, with her gray hair expertly bunned and a large mole at the center of her forehead that always conjured up the phrase, 'hairy eyeball'. Like many pronouncements his mother made, the listener was supposed to believe them without any supporting proof, as if the chain-smoking, bird-thin, gutter-mouthed woman sitting with her spindly legs tightly crossed as she read the newspaper, had at some point in time rivaled Jean Harlow. She was the 'Mission Accomplished' of her time.

'I'll tell you what, Martin.' Evie switched her cigarette to the side of her mouth. It bobbed as she talked, a thin line of smoke snaking from her blackened, right nostril. 'I was fucking gorgeous in my day.'

'I bet you were.' *By 'day' you must mean the Mesozoic era.*

She sniffed the air, as if her sense of smell had not been burned away by forty years of Kool Lights. 'You haven't been drinking, have you?'

He took a deep breath and slowly let it go before answering. 'No, Mother. I haven't been drinking.'

She looked disappointed, as he had known she would. Having been banned from her church group for causing a split in the Ladies' Hospital Auxiliary, ('Like their shit don't smell!') she had lately taken to perusing the personal ads in hopes of finding some new group to which she could belong. She was desperate to have Martin come down with a horrible disease or become addicted to a substance – illegal or otherwise – which had a support group, preferably something close by because she wasn't allowed to drive at night. She had started leaving her various medications out on the kitchen counter, as if to tempt him.

'Look here,' she said, pointing to an ad. 'There's a PFLAG meeting on Lawrenceville Highway.' She looked at him over the paper, eyebrow raised in hopeful expectation.

Martin felt his soul wither like a biodegradable packing peanut in a puddle of water. PFLAG was a support group for parents and friends of gays and lesbians.

'Says here that they serve refreshments.' Her eyes began to sparkle. 'Do you think that means snack foods, too?' She cackled at a thought. 'I bet you they have lady fingers.'

Martin summoned an ounce of dignity from some deep, secret place. 'I am not gay, Mother.'

She stared at him, as if in challenge.

'No.'

She snapped a crease out of the paper. 'Very well,' she quipped. 'What would it matter? It's not like you've been laid in the last ten years.'

Martin spread a thin layer of cholesterol-lowering fake butter on to his waffle. It floated on the top of the ridges like lotion on a dead man.

To someone not intimate with Martin's private life (and in all honesty, but for Evie, that meant everyone), the fact that he knew what lotion looked like on a dead man would have seemed an odd detail needing further explanation. But Martin was late for work, and he did not like to think about his father because it only brought out the spinning spool of 'what ifs' that, quite quickly, tied him up in knots.

What if his father had been around during Martin's formative years to take the brunt of Evie's hounding?

What if his father had been there to talk to Martin about puberty, instead of Evie tossing him a bottle of Vaseline Intensive Care and telling him not to get it on the couch?

What if his father's death had been ruled an accident?

Martin considered these things as he retrieved his briefcase and car keys from the hall table. He checked his tie in the mirror, straightening the knot, trying not to notice the way his chin wattled. He gave in, checking over his shoulder to make sure Evie was still in the kitchen before pinching back the skin on either side, pulling it toward his ears to tighten it up against the jawbone. He studied himself, his turkey giblet gone, and wondered if anyone would ever be able to see past his myriad flaws and know the real Martin – the gentle soul, the book lover, the accountant with stunning accuracy who possessed an unnatural talent for explicating actuarial data.

'Are you still here?' his mother bellowed.

Are you still breathing?

'I'm leaving now,' Martin answered, dropping the skin, watching it settle back into a pouch reminiscent of a seagull's. He rummaged in the closet for a jacket, trying to find one that did not smell of his mother – an olfaction of cigarettes and White Diamonds perfume with a yeasty undertone of string cheese. He held each to his nose and picked the less offensive pea coat. As he buttoned himself up, Martin glanced back at the mirror, catching his profile.

He had not been altogether honest when he'd claimed not to covet all things George Clooney. He could not have the man's grace or charm, but through the magic of plastic surgery, he had managed to swipe his nose. Three years ago, Martin had sprung for a nose job with the plan of addressing his chin in a follow-up operation. The rhinoplasty had proved successful; however, the reaction he had gotten at work was disastrous. His old schoolmates had grown up with Martin and his nose. He had not been called 'Beak' his entire life for nothing. The fact that the beak in question was no longer there seemed to make the nickname even more appropriate. The taunting had gotten worse after the bandages came off, and though he had insisted the operation was to correct a deviated septum, no one had believed him. Chin surgery seemed an invitation to further ridicule after that.

But Martin would be late for work if he took the time to count the many travesties of his life.

He locked the front door after him and walked down the porch stairs. His Camry was parked by the mailbox, the 'twat' scratched into the passenger's side door glinting with morning dew. The insurance adjuster had said the paperwork for repairing the paint would take time to process. Ben Sabatini, the adjuster, had been one of Martin's chief tormentors in high school. Martin was under the impression that the man was deliberately taking his time.

The vandalism had occurred last week. Martin had left the house, much as he was doing this morning, only to find his car had been defiled. Evie's laughter still gurgled in his ear as he thought about the incident.

The policeman who took the report had stated, 'Obviously, this was done by someone who knows you.'

Martin switched his briefcase to his other hand as he walked down the driveway. A light rain started to fall, tickling the end of his nose. He looked at the flowers in the yard – strangely, Evie was an excellent gardener. The front lawn was bordered by all kinds of exotic blooms. Before the gardening club had asked her to leave, then kicked her out, Evie had been the top ribbon-holder in the state for her colorful peonies.

Martin used his key to unlock the Camry by hand (he had read somewhere that remote-key unlocking caused testicular cancer) and tossed his briefcase into the back seat. He was halfway in the car when he noticed that something was wrong with the front end. Slowly, he walked round and saw that the bumper had practically been ripped off.

'Damn,' he mumbled. He glanced back at the house and saw the curtain twitch in the front room. Unbidden, Evie's laughter filled his ears.

'Of course it was done by someone who knows him,' she had told the cop who had taken the report. 'Have you ever seen a bigger twat in your life?'

He was not up for another humiliating police report and Ben Sabatini had stopped returning his calls on the 'twat'. There was no reason to believe this time would be any different. With both hands, Martin pulled on the plastic bumper, bending the hanging piece back and forth until it snapped in two. He did not notice the blood on his hands until he put the damaged bumper in the trunk. Thin lines, almost like paper cuts, criss-crossed his palms. Martin took his handkerchief out of his pocket and wiped his hands. He did not need to look at the house to know that his mother was watching.

Had he not read Tom Clancy shortly after re-reading *Fatal Vision*, the blood on Martin's hands might have triggered the memory that Jeffrey MacDonald, the subject of that true-crime classic, had been convicted of massacring his entire family based on the blood evidence found at the scene of the crime. Instead, his mind was filled with visions of Clancy hero Jack Ryan assassinating the more than likely drunken hood who had slammed into the front bumper of Martin's Camry.

Glancing over his shoulder for snipers, Martin opened the door and got into the car.

We Meet Martin's Co-Workers, or the Hell
That is Martin's Working Life

Southern Toilet Supply had started as a family business almost sixty years ago. Over the years, the Southern compound had spread from a single metal building to a large, modern factory. In the late nineties, a German company had bought the plant. Spreckels Reinigungsmittel und Papier was also a family-owned company, though they treated their new families about as well as Evie treated Martin, which was to say they fired half the staff the day after the papers were signed. The Germans seldom showed up in person, but they sent daily missives to Norton Shaw, demanding higher results in broken English.

'Why is it so that the 2300 cannot reach with the higher levels of salesmanship?'

It had to be said that industrial-sized toilet paper rolls were not a hard sell, but the standards of the Southern Superroll 2300 were not the same as a Scott 500 or, the gold standard in public toilet supply, the Georgia Pacific 2-92. Users of the 2300 often reported early breakage in the first wipe, followed by catastrophic breakdowns in subsequent wiping. Test groups had quit in the middle, forgoing their fifty dollars for want of better hygiene. This hadn't been an issue during the early days of toilet supply. No one had yet done the math to realize that the thinner the paper, the more squares you had to use. While this had proved to be a winning scenario for Southern for many years, lately the customer had started catching on. Why spend eight dollars on a cheap roll of paper that lasts one day when you can spend ten on one that lasts for two?

Even the bathrooms at Southern Toilet Supply did not use their own product, a fact which Martin knew because his desk was conveniently located by the women's bathroom and he saw them taking their own rolls in and out, right under management's eye. Martin had never been a tattler, so he kept his mouth shut. As a matter of fact, he kept his mouth shut about a lot of things he saw happening in the office, most of which would have gotten any number of his tormentors fired. Such was his lot in life: he was too noble for his own good.

He slowed the Camry as he pulled up to the gate. The security guard sat in his little booth watching the morning news. Martin caught a whiff of marijuana as he drove by the open window, but he kept his eyes trained ahead, looking for a parking space amongst the sea of pick-up trucks and SUVs. When he had first bought his Camry someone had remarked that it looked like the new girl on the football team.

Martin's hands had stopped bleeding on the short ride to work. He put a corner of his handkerchief into his mouth to wet it, then wiped some of the blood off the steering wheel. The faux leather would not yield. He would have to get some kind of cleaner. Southern CleanAway was rated for cleaning up biohazards. He would get one of the sample bottles and take care of the mess after lunch.

'Lunch,' he mumbled. He had forgotten to bring his bag lunch.

Martin got out of the car and used the key to lock the door. Then, he saw his briefcase was still in the car, so he unlocked it again.

'Hey, Beak!'

Martin felt his shoulders rise up.

'Beak!' Daryl Matheson had been greeting Martin in this manner every morning since third grade, when Martin had first transferred into Tucker Elementary School. His father had just died, forcing Evie to move the family to a less desirable part of town. Martin had fantasized that his new school would offer new opportunities for friendship and popularity unfathomable at his previous school.

Martin was wrong.

'Beak? Hey, Beak? What's up?'

He would keep calling until Martin answered him. According to *Taking the Bully by the Horns*, this was a recognizable pattern. Daryl did not want to be openly disliked because it would mean that he was a bad person. So long as Martin responded to him, Daryl could continue his fantasy that a 36-year-old man who lived with his mother enjoyed being called 'Beak'.

'Beak? Beak, what up? What's going on, man?'

'Hey, Daryl,' Martin said. Daryl flashed a satisfied smile and punched him in the arm so hard that Martin dropped his briefcase. Papers scattered and Martin grabbed for them, trying to keep the order.

Daryl squatted down, but made no effort to help. 'You've got blood on your hands.'

Martin realized that he was right. The cuts from the plastic bumper had opened up again. He reached for his handkerchief, but remembered he had shoved it in the glove compartment of the car.

Martin muttered, 'What a mess,' as he tried to stack the pages without transferring blood on to them. He saw graphs and pie charts, his grueling work for his presentation at the Toilet Supply Industry Trade Show made visible.

Daryl moved on to more interesting things. 'Damn, man, somebody hit your car.'

'I know.'

'The whole half of the front bumper is missing.'

'I know.'

'That's going to be expensive. Worse than the "twat", even. Hey, when are you gonna get that fixed?'

Martin felt one of his back molars move as he bit down too hard.

'Beak?' Daryl was squatting in front of the bumper. He was dressed in gray coveralls, his name emblazoned in red script over his heart.

Daryl worked on the assembly line as a quality checker. Every tenth bottle of Urine-B-Gone had to be spray-tested. For eight hours a day, the man grabbed bottles and pumped their triggers until a thin stream of blue liquid shot out, and yet Martin – who worked in an office and had to wear ties to work – was considered the loser.

'I filed a report,' he lied. He shoved the rest of the papers into his briefcase. 'The police are taking these injustices very seriously.'

'You know who you should use?' Daryl stood as Martin did. 'Ben Sabatini. He got me fixed real good on my truck. Remember I scraped against that tree and it cut a line into the paint? He had me fixed up the next day. Got one'a them Chrysler 500s as a loaner. Damn, them things are sweet! Ben even worked it so I didn't have to pay my deductible.'

Martin stood there. He really didn't know what to say. 'We should get to work.'

'Yeah,' Daryl agreed. 'Let me know if you need Ben's number. Best guy in the business.'

'Thank you,' Martin responded, gripping his briefcase handle so hard that he felt sweat dripping down his fingers.

Daryl glanced down at Martin's hand. 'You're bleeding again, man.'

'Yeah,' Martin agreed. 'I'll take care of it.'

The two men split – Daryl toward the factory entrance, Martin toward the front office. Instead of going to his desk, Martin went to the men's room. He washed his hands, wondering what kind of diseases the open wounds were exposing him to. The employees were expected to clean up after themselves, so the resulting lack of cleanliness was unsurprising.

He found a bottle of CleanAway in a cabinet by the door. Martin sprayed some on to a paper towel and tried to clean the handle of his briefcase. To his dismay, the leather started to come off. He stopped rubbing immediately, but the chemical kept eating into the handle. He was reminded of a beetle on a corpse as the fake leather started to peel back, exposing the bone white of the plastic underneath. This would have been fascinating but for the fact that Martin had paid almost three hundred dollars for the briefcase.

Tentatively, he touched the exposed edge of the plastic handle. It was sharp as a knife, able to make a thin surface cut into the pad of his finger.

Martin watched blood seep out from the flesh. Death from a thousand cuts.

Martin had never been good at cursing, despite Evie's excellent example. He mumbled under his breath as he left the bathroom and walked through the factory floor, briefcase held close to his chest with both arms. The machinery was not yet running, so he could hear his footsteps echoing around him. He took a detour down a long row of shelving to avoid Daryl, past the stacks of plastic Sani-Lady sanitary disposal units, then went out the back door.

There was a bubbling stream behind the building, tall trees swaying in the wind. During his early years at Southern, Martin had often come out here for a break, taking advantage of the solitude. Now that there was no smoking allowed in the building, that small slice of peace was gone. This was where everyone went during their breaks, as evidenced by the thousands of cigarette butts that littered the concrete. A dilapidated picnic table had two coffee cans full of more cigarette butts. Martin had proposed several weeks ago that a section of the area be cordoned off for non-smokers. His suggestion had been met with the type of ridicule he had come to expect. His insistence that the suggestion box was meant to be anonymous had only made them laugh harder.

The Dumpster was usually overflowing, so he was surprised to find that it had been emptied. Martin opened the briefcase and took out his report, two pens, his business cards and a yellow legal pad, all of which he placed on the only semi-clean part of the concrete he could find. He tried to open the Dumpster's metal door, but it was rusted shut. The top was at least four feet above his head. Martin glanced around, then spread his legs and tossed the briefcase granny-style into the air. It went straight up, then straight back down. He nearly tripped over his own feet to get out of the way as it hurtled toward his face. Martin cursed and tried again, pushing up on the corners, trying to concentrate his aim. This time, the briefcase ended up at his feet, the corner collapsing against the concrete.

He stood there, hands on his hips, feeling a lifetime of failure starting to bubble up into his chest as he stared at the briefcase on the ground. It wasn't just that he'd been duped into paying leather prices for a vinyl. It was the 'twat' on his car. It was the damaged bumper. It was Daryl calling him Beak, and his mother's Munchausen by gay Proxy.

Martin kicked the briefcase. The release felt so good that he kicked it again. Soon, he was jumping up and down on the briefcase, smashing it to pieces. He scooped up the mangled case and slammed it into the side of the Dumpster several times before exhaustion took over. Martin bent at the waist, panting. He was sweating in his pea coat. Rivulets of perspiration slid down his back.

The door opened. One of the line workers stood there, a cigarette in her mouth, lighter in her hands. They had never been formally introduced, yet the woman felt familiar enough with him to ask, 'What the hell are you doing?'

'Mind your own darn' business,' he said, scooping up the pieces of the broken case. He glanced up at the Dumpster, but did not dare try another attempt with a witness. He picked up his report and the other items, then walked around the building. Several minutes later, he found himself at his car. He unlocked the trunk and put the tattered briefcase beside the broken bumper. Martin looked up at the cloudy, gray sky. Two strikes already and it wasn't even nine o'clock. What could possibly be the third?

Suddenly, the clouds moved, a ray of sun peeking out. Martin closed his eyes against the light. Without warning, the joyful tones of the Harlem Gospel Choir filled his ears. ' "Lord, lift me *up*! Take me *hi-yi-yi-igher*!" '

The singing abruptly stopped as the engine was cut on the black Monte Carlo that had pulled up beside Martin's Camry.

'Whatchu doin', fool?' Unique Jones slammed the car door, her keys jingling in one hand, a tall Dunkin' Donuts mocha latte in the other. Her purse was the size of a feed sack; the strap cut into the fleshy part of her exposed shoulder. Despite the chill in the air, she was wearing a tight-fitting, bright orange sundress with matching orange shoes. Unique was a large black woman who liked to offset her dark skin with colorful scarves and glittery fingernail polish. Sometimes, she wore a turban around her head. Other days, she let her intricately braided hair dangle around her shoulders. She had terrified Martin from the day she had first walked into the building.

Martin stammered, 'I-I-I—'

'Hush up, doughboy. We got work to do.'

She talked to him like she was his boss, when

in fact the opposite was true. The only time she had shown him any respect was when she had interviewed for the job. 'It's Unique with an accent on the "e",' she had politely corrected him. Martin had glanced down at her application where she had written her name, Unique Jones, wondering which 'e' she could mean. He was befuddled. Was it French? Jo-naise, perhaps?

'You-nee-kay,' she had explained, laughing, 'That's all right, baby, nobody gets it at first, but once they do, they never forget.'

He had smiled at her, thinking that this was the first time he had been called 'baby' without the implicit pejorative. One of the few things Martin could remember about his father was a joke he liked to tell: How do you catch a unique rabbit? *Unique* up on it.

This Unique was a high school drop-out who hadn't even bothered to get her GED. She had one month from a secretarial school under her belt and two months of accounting school. 'I learned everything I needed,' she told him. 'You either got it up here or you don't.' She tapped her temple on this last part, and Martin noticed the gold dollar-sign appliqué on the glossy red fingernail of her index finger.

'We're doing a lot of interviews,' he told her, which was actually a lie. He had reserved the office conference room weeks ago when he placed the ad, expecting back-to-back interviews. He had read up on *Interviews for Dummies* so he could ask salient questions such as, 'What are some of your best features?' or, 'If I asked a close friend to name one of your flaws, what would it be?'

The only other applicant had been a man who had shown up an hour late and yelled at Martin that he could not be expected to punch a time-clock; a startling statement, considering that none of the office staff were expected to clock in.

'How many interviews you got?' Unique asked.

'Well, I . . . uh . . .' Martin felt his throat work as he swallowed. 'Many. Several-many.' He pronounced the words as if they were hyphenated, and she had narrowed her eyes as if she could see straight into his soul.

She had shaken her head. 'Nuh-uh,' she insisted. 'You're going to give me the job now. I can't go home and wait by the phone. I got other responsibilities.'

'I just—'

'What time you want me to show up? Don't say eight, 'cause this kind of beautiful don't happen without a little help in the morning. You know what I mean?' She had flicked back her braided hair on that last remark. The way the beads rattled against each other reminded Martin of the time he had found a rattlesnake in his bunk at summer camp. Granted, it turned out to be a fake (a revelation unfortunately not reached before Martin had alerted the entire compound to the dangerous creature), but the beads in its tail rattled the same.

She was fishing around in her purse for her keys as Martin tried to explain that all front office employees were expected to be at their desks by eight-thirty sharp. 'I'll see you around nine on Friday,' she told him, standing. 'I gotta take off early, though, 'cause my niece is in town. All right? I'll see ya then.'

She was gone before he could answer, her half-empty Dunkin' Donuts mocha latte leaving a ring on the conference-room table. Her scent still filled the room – a sickly sweet concoction like candy floss and Coca-Cola that competed with the disturbing, yeasty odor that had come as she uncrossed her legs. This lady fug was what had stuck with Martin, and he caught a whiff of it even now as Unique headed across the parking lot.

'You gonna get that "twat" off your car?' she asked.

Martin had to jog to keep up with her. For a large woman, she moved with amazing speed.

'I've put a call into—'

'Sabatini ain't gonna help you, fool. He was laughing so hard when he came out here I half expected a brick to drop out of his pants.'

Martin remained silent. The brick comment, he felt, was completely unnecessary.

'You need to call his boss.'

She was always telling him what to do. Most of her sentences started with 'you need to.' God forbid Martin tell *her* that she needed to do something. He was senior to her in every way, yet Unique was the one who took control in the office – bringing in potted plants, scattering candles, air fresheners and photos of her lap dog around the common areas.

Granted, she was a faster typist, and she tended not to make very many mistakes, but she hardly had it the same as he did with her job of invoicing and collections for non-liquid products and vending items. You couldn't really compare Vomit-Up granules and LadyTickler condoms to the massive roll-paper orders and toilet-seat liners that Martin processed. It was apples and oranges, as he often told Norton Shaw.

To make matters worse, she had despicable work habits. From the moment she showed up, she would keep her cellphone to one ear and the business phone to the other. She would cross-talk to her sister, who worked in a church office, with customers listening on the other line. Meanwhile, her glossy fingernails would click-click-click against the keys like a Chihuahua on a tile floor while her hair rat-tat-tatted like a rubber snake with beads in its tail. About sixty times a day, she would apply lotion to her hands, and oftentimes her feet. The one time Martin politely asked her to find a more appropriate place to oil up, she had screamed, 'I can't help it I'm ashy!' and that was that.

As a large-breasted woman with a generous waistline, she had to maneuver herself carefully around the desk. Martin had been intrigued at first to watch the alignment of breast, stomach and arm that made it possible for her to reach the computer keyboard. She had misinterpreted his scientific interest as unbridled lust, admonishing, 'Honey, you ain't got the stamina to ring this bell!' Then, he'd had to listen to her relay the story to her sister, whose 'amen' could be heard across the room.

These were not isolated incidents but daily occurrences. Martin lived in terror of her pronouncements, which were usually made in mixed company during the most inopportune moments. He would be going over a time card with one of the shift workers and she would shoot out a, 'You ain't following what he's saying, fool!' Or, Norton Shaw would come down to check on receivables and she would shout, 'He got some bad gas from lunch. Let's do this outside.'

At times, she reminded him of the Geraldine doll his mother had bought him for Christmas when he was a child. Flip Wilson was one side while Geraldine, his cross-dressing alter ego, was on the other. Pull the cord and witticisms would come out, such as 'The Devil made me do it!' and 'When you're hot, you're hot!'

Perhaps worst of all, and even more humiliating than listening to her complain to her sister about menstrual cramps while she took off her shoes and lotioned her feet, was that she kept promoting herself. On her first day, Martin had foolishly given Unique the ability to order her own business cards. In the course of three years, her title had changed from 'accounting assistant', to 'accounts executive' to 'senior account executive'. Any day now, he fully expected to find a card that read, 'Unique Jones, Chief Financial Officer'.

Meanwhile, Martin's own cards simply read, 'Accounting'. He had ordered a thousand printed up his first day of work. Sixteen years had passed and the box was still half-full.

Back in the parking lot, Unique had stopped at the front door. 'Your mama didn't teach you to open the door for a lady?'

Martin was opening the door for her as a witty comeback occurred, but she was halfway to her desk by the time his mouth moved to get it out.

She said, 'Don't mumble, fool,' as she tossed her purse on to the desk. The chair made a noise like two pool balls hitting against each other as she sat.

Martin quietly put his stack of business cards, his pens, the yellow legal pad and his report on his own desk. His chair made no noise as he sat down and turned on his computer. When he'd first started working at Southern, the only automated part of the process was an IBM Selectric that got stuck on the 'g' and the 'l' no matter how many times it was cleaned. All the ledgers had been done by hand – Martin's hand. People from the factory floor were in and out of his office all day, giving Martin a quick wave or a smile. Mr Cordwell, the owner, would occasionally drop in and talk to him about fishing or taking the family out on the lake that weekend. Martin would nod, then Mr Cordwell would go to the bathroom (the only entrance was through Martin's office), and then he'd come back again and toss the paper towel he'd used to dry his hands on to Martin's desk. They were heady times, the Cordwell days – peaceful times. That was before the Germans came in and made Martin hire an assistant. It was never the same with the old man gone.

Before Unique, he'd had his desk on the far wall, away from the toilets (she had changed that the first day). The view was better over there because you could see out the window to the factory floor. It gave you some sense of being part of a group. At times, Martin had glanced up and seen them all standing at their stations and thought, 'Ah, my colleagues.' Now, he kept his head down for fear of Unique misinterpreting his glance and shouting, 'Don't even think about it, fool. You ain't got the vocabulary to read this book!'

Unique was staring at him. 'I asked you a question, Fool.'

'What?' Martin asked, painfully aware that he had become so accustomed to being addressed as 'Fool'. He was even beginning to think of it as a proper noun.

'I said, where is Sandy?'

Martin glanced out the window. The stairs leading up to the executive office were empty. Usually, Sandy came down to use the bathroom and check in with Unique before work started. It was odd that she wasn't here, especially since last night's episode of *Dancing With the Stars* had been particularly competitive. Even the judges had been shocked.

Unique craned her neck, trying to see up the stairs. 'Who's that?'

Martin was thinking the same thing. He saw a foot appear at the top of the stairs. It was clad in a white tennis shoe. His gaze followed tan hose up the calf to a below-the-knee beige skirt. Who did that calf belong to? A beauty queen? A salesperson from a pulp goods distributor? The woman started to walk down the stairs, and he was reminded of the beautiful passage from *The Great Gatsby* when we first meet Mrs Wilson . . . '*She was in the middle thirties, and faintly stout, but she carried her surplus flesh sensuously as some women can.*'

'Uh-oh,' Unique said. 'This ain't good.'

'*Her face . . . contained no facet or gleam of beauty, but there was an immediately perceptible vitality about her as if the nerves of her body were continually smoldering.*'

'What's wrong with you, Fool?'

Martin became aware that his mouth was hanging open.

'That's the police.'

Unique pronounced the word with two syllables: po-lice. Martin glanced around the room at the boxes stacked high to the ceiling as if he could detect some theft. Southern had been broken into once before. In 1996, just before the Olympics, hooligans had busted the back door and papered the entire factory floor. Martin had been the first to discover the crime; he could still remember the sense of abject violation he'd felt as he'd picked 2300 from the machinery. Had it happened again? Who had dared to target Southern Toilet Supply this time? What rapscallion had breached the sanctity of a small American business that was owned by a multi-national conglomerate?

On the stairs, he saw that there was a man behind the woman, a gray-haired, square shoulders kind of guy who probably wore cologne and winked a lot to make his point. Rounding up the end of the group was Norton Shaw, whose face was scrunched up like a fist.

'Uh-oh,' Unique repeated. 'Norton don't look happy.'

Martin was standing, his fists clenched. Who had attacked this simple little business? What had they done this time?

The door opened. The woman stood there, light pouring in all around her. Her blonde hair had been permed too much, or perhaps the winter weather had split the ends. There were tiny splotches of dry skin on her face and what looked like the last throes of a pimple in the crevice of her right nostril. She was older than he had first guessed, probably in her late forties, which somehow made her more beautiful (even as a boy, Martin had always been attracted to older women). There was just something about her – some kind of inner beauty, an air of knowing – that commanded attention.

She took in the office, the stacked boxes, the potted succulents. Behind her, the man asked, 'Are you the twat?'

Unique barked a laugh that made Martin's eardrums hurt. 'That's him. That Fool over there.' She pointed a long red fingernail his way.

Norton Shaw gave Martin a wary glance before turning around and wordlessly heading back up the stairs.

The woman took a wallet out of her jacket pocket. She flipped it open to show Martin a gold badge. 'I'm Anabahda.'

Martin squinted at the ID above her badge, trying to put words to the sounds he had heard. She closed the wallet too fast, though.

'This is Detective Bruce Benedict, my partner.'

The man winked at Martin, but his focus was squarely on Unique, taking in every inch of her. She smiled at his attention, practically batting her eyelashes. With his slicked-back hair, expensive suit and purple silk tie, he reminded Martin of a character from a Stuart Woods novel. And, like the typical Woodsian character, he carried himself as if every woman he met wanted to give him a blowjob.

'You're Martin Reed?' Anabahda asked.

'Yes.' He added, 'ma'am' to let her know he respected her authority. 'Are you here about my car? I hope you've caught the vandal.'

'Why don't we go somewhere and talk? Your boss said we could use the conference—'

'You got a card?' Unique interrupted.

Martin smiled at Anabahda. 'You'll have to excuse—'

'Fool, these are detectives. They don't send detectives when somebody twats up your car.' She snapped her fingers at Benedict. 'Gimme your card.'

The man gave his partner a knowing, lopsided smile as he handed his card to Unique.

'Homicide!' she screamed, nearly falling out of her chair. 'Martin, you don't talk to Homicide cops. My cousin talked to them once and he got sent to jail for twenty years!'

Anabahda asked, 'What's your cousin's name?'

Unique's face went blank. She picked up her

purse. 'I think I left my oven on.' She scampered out the door, only the lingering scent of garlic and mocha latte indicating she had even been there.

Martin swallowed. He was alone with her now, except for Benedict. 'Can I see your card, please?'

She took out her wallet again and dug around in one of the pockets. 'This is just routine questioning, Mr Reed. There's no reason to worry.'

He took the card, electric shocks going through his body when his fingers brushed against hers. Martin noticed that she chewed her cuticles, just like he did.

'Mr Reed?'

He realized he was staring at her. Martin ducked down his head, reading the card: Detective Anther 'An' Albada, Homicide Division. 'An' not 'Anne' or 'Ann' but 'An'. The simplicity was breathtaking, yet alluring. And the Albada . . . how exotic, how foreign . . . He wanted to touch the raised letters to see if the tingling sensation came back.

'Mr Reed?' She was leaning against Unique's desk, arms crossed over her chest. He saw a gold Timex on her wrist – spare, utilitarian, just like the lady.

She looked tired. He wondered what it might feel like to have her put her head in his lap. Martin blushed at the thought, thinking that, if she could read his mind, she would assume that his wanting her head in his lap had sexual connotations, which was not the case – he simply wanted to stroke her hair, to ask her about her day. Maybe he would make her fishsticks and Tater Tots (Martin's favorite meal), and then when the kids came home, he would help them with their homework and then carry her to bed where they would make sweet, gentle love and she would look into his eyes and—

'Mr Reed?'

Martin looked back at her. 'Yes, ma'am?'

'Can you tell us where you were yesterday?'

'At work.'

'I mean, after work.'

'I took my mother to the Peony Club. She left her good trowel.'

'And then what?'

Martin felt his face flush. His throat tightened. He had taken his mother home, and then he had done something awful – so awful that the words strangled in his throat. The *one time* someone asked him what he had done the night before, and he had actually *done* something, but he could not talk about it. At least not to this beautiful flower of a woman. Oh, the irony! The unseemliness of it all!

The toilet flushed. All of them turned their heads, surprised by the noise. Daryl Matheson was zipping up his coveralls as he came into the office, saying, 'Shit, Marty, gimme the spray. Something dead just crawled outta my—' He stopped when he saw Martin's guests. 'What are the cops doing here?'

Martin opened his bottom desk drawer and fetched the OdorOutter (one of Southern's most popular sellers). 'They're here about my car,' Martin told him. 'Be sure to tell Ben Sabatini that when you see him next.'

Daryl shook the spray can and headed back into the bathroom. The office was so quiet they could hear the spraying and subsequent coughing. Martin held his breath (Southern had settled a civil suit out of court with a customer who claimed that OdorOutter ate away the lining of her esophagus) and smiled at An.

Daryl came back out of the toilet, waving his hand in the air to fight the fumes. His voice cracked when he spoke. 'Damn, sorry about that, folks.' He coughed a few times, then a few more. Then even more. Martin shot an apologetic look to An as he plucked some tissues out of the Kleenex box on his desk and handed them to Daryl.

'Jesus!' Daryl choked. He cleared his throat a few times, spit in the tissue, then handed it back to Martin. 'Thanks, man.' He wiped his mouth with the back of his hands and addressed the detective. 'Are y'all here about all that blood on his car?'

Suddenly, the OdorOutter wasn't the only thing sucking breathable air from the room.

An asked, 'What blood on the car?'

Daryl nodded toward Martin. 'This morning. He had blood all over his hands, too. I thought maybe he hit a deer or something, but there was hair on the bumper – like, hair from somebody's head.' He shrugged. 'Then Darla saw him outside by the Dumpster beating the ever-loving Jesus out of his briefcase.' He glanced back at Martin. 'You oughtta talk to somebody about that temper of yours, man.' With that, he left the office.

Martin felt his mouth moving, but no words would come out.

Benedict reached underneath the back of his jacket and pulled out a pair of handcuffs. 'Martin Reed, I am arresting you for the murder of Sandra Burke.'

'Sandy?' he asked, craning his neck to look up the stairs even as Benedict slung him around like a sack of Meyer lemons. Was that why she hadn't come downstairs to talk about *Dancing With the Stars*? 'You don't understand!' Martin tried. 'Why would I hurt Sandy? Why would I hurt anyone?'

'Mr Reed,' An began, 'why don't you clear this up right now and tell us where you were last night?'

Martin gulped, his face reddening again. This was awful, just awful. Hadn't this very thing happened in John Grisham's *The Innocent Man* – some poor shlub in the wrong place at the right time?

'Mr Reed?'

Grisham was a lawyer. He knew how these things worked. In his head, Martin consulted the legal advice contained in his many books. *The Client*. *The Broker*. *The Appeal*. 'I believe,' Martin began, 'I have the right to remain silent.'

Wherein We Learn That There is More to Anther Than Meets the Eye, or An Another Thing

An stared at Martin Reed through the observation mirror. He sat alone in the interview room, his pudgy face squeezed into a ball of fear. The wisps of hair covering his round head reminded her of Charlie Brown. He kept clenching his fists on the table in front of him as if Lucy had yet again tricked him into trying to kick the ball. It was the same kind of clenching he'd been doing when they'd walked into his office – or at least what Martin seemed to think was his office. To An's eye, it looked like a break room that had two desks and was stacked almost wall-to-wall with boxed payables and receivables from the last fifteen years. If anyone found it odd that the accounting department was basically an adjunct to the toilets, no one was commenting.

Bruce opened the door and came into the room. 'Nothing in his house.'

An had assumed the search of the Reed home would yield little evidence.

'His mother's terrified, says he's been acting strange lately. Might be hitting the bottle again.'

'Again?'

'She says he doesn't like to talk about it. Must be in recovery.' Bruce shrugged; there were lots of cops in recovery. 'The woman's a potty mouth, by the way. Some of the shit outta her mouth made me blush.'

Coming from a man who used 'cunting' as an adjective, that was saying a lot. Of course, An couldn't talk. She was quite explicit around prisoners, who tended to respond to threats better than pleasantries.

Bruce continued, 'You should see his bedroom. Wall-to-wall books with more in boxes in the garage. We're talking tens of thousands of them. The guy must read all the time.'

An studied Martin. He didn't strike her as the cerebral type. 'What kinds of books?'

'Thrillers mostly. James Patterson, Vince Flynn – that kind of stuff.'

An couldn't say anything. She refused to

answer her phone when a Columbo movie was on. Not that it rang much, but she was constantly being surveyed for her opinion on things. Talk to those people once and they never gave up. 'Did the mother give him an alibi for last night?'

'She said he took her on an errand, then they went home, then he went out and she didn't see him until she woke up this morning.'

An nodded, processing the information. Through the mirror, she could see Martin's mouth moving as he mumbled to himself.

'What a tool,' Bruce commented.

An could not disagree, but was this tool a murderer?

Bruce seemed to read her mind. 'We've got Reed's blood mixed in with the victim's on both the front bumper and in the trunk.'

'You saw his hands. What he said about the cuts would explain the blood.'

'If he's innocent, why'd he clean off his briefcase with acid?'

She allowed, 'Maybe he's more dastardly than he looks.'

'He's got a crush on you.'

'Please.' Men didn't get crushes on Anther. She was hardly a sultry siren.

'Listen, you could work that angle. Make him think he's got a chance. Guy like that probably hasn't seen a pussy since he was being born outta one.'

An did not respond to the comment. She had been a cop for almost twenty years now. Early on, she'd made a habit of challenging every sexist remark or disgusting joke uttered by her mostly male colleagues. This had done nothing but garner the reputation that she was a lesbian. When she had insisted that she was not, in fact, homosexual, they chastised her for being ashamed of her sexuality. When she had pointed out that (at the time) she was married, they had sadly shaken their heads, as if to ask to what lengths she would go in her denial of the love that dare not speak its name. An had been so maligned over the years that, in order to protect herself – really, in order to properly perform her job – she had fallen into the habit of fabrication.

Fabrication. That was a pretty word to use for a lie. An was not by nature a liar. Her father had detested lies and taught her early on that the punishment for a lie was much more harsh than the punishment for confession. And yet, here she was, fabricating to her heart's content. And her heart *was* content, though only when she let herself slip into believing her own stories.

This was how it happened: Charlie, her husband, had just died. This was fifteen years ago. There was no one at home to cook for, no laundry to do, no shirts to iron. A big case had just been solved – a child killer was going to the electric chair. People were in a celebratory mood. An decided that she would go to the local cop bar and have a drink with her fellow brothers in blue.

They all got drunk, but An was better at holding her liquor. Or, maybe she wasn't. Somebody hit on her. Somebody made a comment not to bother. Somebody called her a dyke. Somebody called her frigid. Maybe it was the word 'frigid,' because that was what Charlie called her when, for some crazy reason, she didn't want to have sex with him after he'd beaten her.

No matter how it happened, that was when Jill was born.

Jill was a nurse who worked with children. She was a kind and caring woman. She had just been diagnosed with breast cancer. She was the love of An's life. She was dying. They all felt sorry for her. They all shut up.

The next morning, An woke up with a

throbbing headache. When she got to work, everyone was quiet, respectful. A few asked how Jill was doing. 'Jill?' she had echoed, and then it had hit her, the half-drunk fabrications from the night before. She'd tucked her head down, mumbled, 'I don't really want to talk about it,' and ran to the women's room where she cleaned out her purse, filed her nails and took a nap, only to emerge to concerned stares and 'chin ups' from her new friends.

Belonging to a group was an alien concept to An. Not that she had never had friends, but as the daughter of Dutch immigrants, she had never quite fitted in. During the summers, when most girls were off at camp, she was visiting relatives in Hindeloopen, walking along the narrow streets and wooden bridges of her seafaring ancestors, still never quite fitting in with her 'y'alls' and 'fixin' tos'. Her parents fared no better. Like many immigrants before them, they had come to America seeking a new life. As with those earlier immigrants, the life they made for themselves was basically the same as the one they had back home, but in a different country. They attended parties for the Dutch–American Society. They drank Heineken and sucked on coins of *honingdrop* that their relatives back home were kind enough to mail. Most of their friends were childless, Dutch ex-pats, except a few shifty Norwegians who mostly stood in the corner at parties talking among themselves.

Walking into the Albada house, you would never guess that you were still in the American South. An's mother was an art teacher who was passionate about blending substance and style. Every room was colorfully decorated in bright reds, yellows and greens. The dining room was boldly striped in blue. There were cupboards they had brought from home, leafy floral patterns and swirls intricately carved into every inch of wood, then painted in complementary colors. On Halloween, her mother would don her chintz *wentke*, and – solely as a concession to her ignorant art students – put on a pair of wooden clogs she had bought at a tourist stand in Schiphol Airport.

Her father had been overly educated, as was the Dutch way, and he insisted his daughter be the same. When An was not studying, she was working on extra credit projects or helping her father in the lab (Eduart Albada was a botanist for the State of Georgia). He had a small shed in the back yard – her mother called it the *likhus* after the small houses in Hindeloopen where the sea captains' families stayed – and An would spend hours with him there over the weekends, watching his steady, square hands as he grafted together different plants in hopes of creating a tulip that was more resistant to the South's unpredictable seasons.

And so it was that An grew up a much-beloved only child with very few friends her own age. She had never been particularly lonely, or at least she *thought* she'd never been lonely, but what An realized when Jill came into her life was that she had always been alone. Even when she was married to Charlie, there was that sense that she did not quite belong to him, that he did not quite *see* her when she entered a room or asked a question.

But, not anymore. That all stopped the day An walked out of the women's room and was greeted by her colleagues as an equal. When had it happened? When had Jill crossed over from being a figment of An's imagination into a living, breathing part of An's life? It had never occurred to her as she cleaned out loose pieces of paper and various pieces of fuzz from her purse that Jill was taking on real physical aspects in her mind.

Okay, well, An had to admit that she milked it at first. She took some personal time, claiming she wanted to sit with Jill during her treatments, when really it was because she was having bad cramps and there was a John Wayne marathon on TBS. Then, there was the day she overslept and missed an important meeting. Telling them that Jill was sick from chemo and she'd had to take her to the doctor was only a little white lie. What was the point of those stupid meetings anyway? They were cops. They didn't have to be rounded up into a smelly conference room to be told that they needed to catch the bad guys.

Of course, there was no way to get around the fact that it was a whopper of a falsehood when An had taken a week-long trip to Florida under the guise of flying Jill to the Mayo Clinic to see a world-renowned specialist. A handful of people noted her suntan, which An explained away by telling them she insisted on staying with Jill during radiation treatments. Maybe it wasn't so much of a lie, because by then An felt a real connection to Jill. While the thought of lesbian sex wasn't particularly appealing (or even concrete in her mind, because what, exactly, did two women do together?), An liked the idea of the companionship, the connection with another human being.

In short, she fell in love.

Over the ensuing months, the myth of Jill had slowly evolved into a reality. An had worked on the detective squad for three years, but no one had ever bothered to talk to her before Jill had appeared. Knowing that An had a sick lover had somehow humanized her with these men. She made friendships – lifelong relationships. A couple of them had wives who'd had breast cancer. They gave An literature on survivors. Then, one day, they had all surrounded her desk and handed her a sign-up sheet. Real tears had welled into her eyes when she realized that the entire squad had agreed to participate in the Avon Breast Cancer Walk on behalf of Jill.

It was then that she knew that Jill had to die. Too much water had passed under the bridge. An was telling so many stories that she didn't know how to keep up with them anymore. The worst part was that people wanted to meet Jill. They wanted to know this strong woman who had stared death in the face. Oddly enough, the day

An called into work to tell her boss that Jill had passed away (conveniently occurring on the same day that Macy's was having its annual fifty per cent off white sale), she had gotten so choked up that she'd had to hang up the phone.

It hadn't stopped there, really. There were the condolence cards to deal with. The flowers. Of course they'd had an impromptu wake at the same bar where the legend of Jill had been born. They drank to her: the nurse, the friend, the lover. They had sung sad songs and An had told them about the time Jill had saved a homeless man from a burning building and the way she always put toothpaste on An's toothbrush, even at the end when she was so sick she could barely lift her head. She had thought about cheating on Jill once – had she ever told them that? Nothing had happened, but it had been a hard time for them both, and, in the end, An felt like it made them stronger.

The worst part was that An had chosen the name Jill because she enjoyed watching Gillian Anderson on *The X-Files*. Her thick, red hair, her sharp chin and petite waist were all attributes An would have loved for herself. She knew now that basing Jill on a real person was a big mistake.

Sometimes, An would see Anderson, introducing a PBS special or promoting one of her many causes, and would get a lump in her throat, as if she was seeing a ghost from a happier time in her life.

'Hey,' Bruce said. 'You in there?'

An nodded her head. They both stared at Martin, who was mumbling to himself.

'Hard day for you, huh?'

An nodded again. Bruce's mother had died of breast cancer when he was a child. He had brought An flowers this morning, marking the five-year anniversary of Jill's death.

'You had eight good years,' Bruce reminded her. 'That's more than most people get.'

'Yeah.' An fought the sadness that came with the false memories: Jill rubbing her feet; Jill fixing her dinner; Jill running her a bath. (It must be said that many of An's fantasies cast Jill in a decidedly subservient role.)

'I'm here for you, babe.' Bruce patted her shoulder. 'You know that, right?'

His touch was warm, and An flashed back to that crazy night six years ago when she had for some reason let herself fall for the limited charms of Bruce Benedict. They were working hard on a case, and the truth of the matter was that An missed a man's touch. She missed the gruffness, the warmness, the sense of being filled to the brim with a man who knew what he was doing. It had been a horrible, stupid mistake to think that this man would be Bruce (and they had both agreed never to tell Jill; it would've broken her heart).

Bruce dropped his hand. 'I dunno, An, this guy's just creepy. If he didn't do this, he did something.'

She nodded a third time, glad that the focus was back on Martin Reed. The pasty man knew his way around the law. He had refused to talk to them without a lawyer present and insisted that he was not signing any statements unless they were written in his own hand. What kind of game was he playing?

Bruce said, 'You should probably take this. I got no traction with him in the car.'

Possibly because Bruce had noted the fat around Martin's wrists as he'd tightened the handcuffs looked like dough squeezing out of the donut maker at Krispy Kreme.

An chewed her cuticles. She thought about Sandra Burke, the way her broken body had been discarded in a drainage ditch. The car had nearly pulverized the woman. Treadmarks crushed into her brain, squirting gray matter on to the road.

The intercom buzzed behind them. Bruce pressed the button, asking, 'Yeah?'

'Reed's lawyer is here.'

'Be right there.' Bruce opened the door to leave, but An stopped him.

'Give me a couple of minutes with him,' she said, indicating Martin with a tilt of her head.

'Sure.'

'Did you get the crime-scene photos back yet?'

'Should be here any minute.'

'Bring them in with the lawyer. I'm going to see if I can get something out of him.'

Bruce nodded and left, letting the door swing back. One of the downsides of being a pretend lesbian was that men didn't open doors for her anymore.

An pulled back her hair into a loose pony tail as she walked toward the interrogation room. There was a small sliver of glass in the door, and she saw Martin still sitting at the table, still clenching his fists. When she entered the room, he stood up, as if they were in a Jane Austen movie. She expected him to say something like, 'Forsooth', but he just stood there, hands clenched, staring at her with his dark green eyes.

'Please sit down,' she told him, taking the chair opposite. 'Your lawyer is on his way.'

'Does he have any experience?'

An was surprised by the question. 'I don't know,' she admitted.

'Because a lot of times people get court-appointed lawyers who aren't experienced,' Martin told her. 'I've read about it – cases where innocent people get lazy lawyers who are blind, literally blind, as in they can't see. Some of them are even alcoholics or have narcolepsy!'

'Is that so?'

'It's very troubling. There have been many books written about this very thing.'

An had never been a fan of public defenders, but she was a cop, so that was hardly an earth-shattering revelation. 'My experience with public defenders is that you get what you pay for.'

'Just as I suspected. I appreciate your honesty.'

'Is there anything you want to say to me, Mr Reed?'

'Not until my lawyer gets here. I hope you don't think I am being rude, but this is a very serious situation. Do you realize I've never even gotten a speeding ticket?' He shook his head. 'Of course you do. You'll have already pulled my record. Are you searching my house? Is that why this is taking so long? You're trying to get a search warrant?'

'What do you think we'll find in your house?'

He mumbled his answer, but she heard him clearly enough: 'A very angry sixty-three-year-old woman.'

An said, 'Your mother seems to think you're an alcoholic.'

His lips sputtered, 'She wishes!'

An looked down at his hands, which were clasped together on the table. Bruce had left on the handcuffs, and An had to admit he was right about the Krispy Kreme machine. 'Give me your hands,' she said, taking out her keys. She tried not to touch him as she took off the cuffs, but there was no way to get around it. His skin was clammy enough to make her flesh crawl.

'Thank you,' he said, rubbing his wrists to get the blood back into them. 'Albada – is that German?'

'Dutch.'

He affected a very bad accent. '*Pardonnemoi.*'

'That's French.'

'*Oui*.'

'French again.'

He blinked several times.

An sighed. 'Do you want to tell me where you were last night?'

'I told you that I took my mother to get her trowel.'

'Are you aware that your mother has a restraining order filed against her by the Peony Club of Lawrenceville?'

His throat moved as he swallowed. 'It was just a misunderstanding.'

'And what about the Ladies' Hospital Auxiliary?'

His wet lips parted in shock. 'They filed a complaint, too?'

'Did your mother not tell you that?'

He shook his head, obviously agitated.

'They seem to think she's a violent person.'

'She's not violent. She's just . . . intimidating.'

An intimidating mother. That was interesting. 'Has she ever hit you?'

'She threw her shoe at me once, but I think that was more because I was listening to the TV with my headphones on. You know, the wireless kind?' An nodded. 'They were interfering with her hearing aid somehow.'

'So, she threw her shoe at you?'

'Only to get my attention.' He spoke as if this was completely logical. 'What does my mother have to do with any of this?'

'I'm a detective, Mr Reed. I put together clues. What I see in front of me is a man who comes from a violent family. I see someone who drives a car with blood on it – blood that belongs to a dead woman.

'Well, okay, that – I'll admit – does not look good.'

'No, it doesn't.'

'I suppose I fit the profile, don't I?' He started nodding, agreeing with himself. 'A loner who lives with his mother. Over-educated, under-employed.'

Well, he'd lost her on those last two.

'I hope you don't think I am a disorganized killer. I am a very tidy man. Ask my colleague, Unique Jones. She's often commented on my retentiveness.'

An would have liked nothing more than to talk to Unique Jones. The woman had a warrant out on her for shoplifting. The home address she had given Southern Toilet Supply was a vacant lot. 'Are you a killer, Mr Reed?'

'No, of course not!' He seemed offended again. 'I told you what happened to my car this morning, how I cut my hands. I am the victim here. Someone is setting me up.'

'Why would someone set you up?'

'Exactly!' he retorted, driving his index finger into the table as if she had made his point for him.

'Where were you last night, Mr Reed?'

He stared at his hands. The red marks from the cuffs were still visible. She saw a strange-looking purple ridge down the side of his thumb. She had noticed it during booking, and he'd mumbled something about an industrial accident.

Martin asked, 'Is "Anther" Dutch, too?'

'It's the part of a flower where pollen is produced.' She sat back, feeling overwhelmingly tired. 'My father was a botanist. He was hoping for a boy.'

Martin blinked, not understanding.

Well, it wasn't her best joke, but she didn't think it was as bad as his reaction implied. Then again, the man was sitting in a police interrogation room being questioned about his involvement in a brutal murder, so perhaps she was expecting too much.

One of the reasons Charlie, her dead husband, had gotten so mad at An was that he didn't quite get her sense of humor. He would admonish her for her smart mouth, accuse her of lording her education over him (as if a bachelor's degree in art history was anything to write home about). He would start off low, like one of those sirens you crank by hand, and the more things would spin out of control, the louder he would get, until he was on top of her, screaming, his fists pounding into her body – but never her face.

It was embarrassing, really, to be a 23-year-old woman who put on a uniform and gun every day to keep the peace, only to have the pulp beaten out of her almost every night. She never fought back, though surely Charlie deserved it. What was it about An's nature that made her seem like a victim? She saw domestic violence so much at work that it seemed almost commonplace. Those early years on the force, half of her calls were because some man had gotten drunk and taken it out on a woman. Her eyes would glaze over at their stories of love, the excuses they made. And then she would go home and Charlie would beat her.

Really, it was luck that he'd slipped in the bathtub and hit his head. When An had found him there, the only question in her mind was whether to leave the water running or not while he slowly bled to death. She was the child of Dutch parents, and knew better than to waste water. She had turned off the shower, then gone in to watch *Wheel of Fortune*.

This was back when you had to buy merchandise with your winnings. An could still remember the woman who had won that night. The camera panned over all the exotic, expensive items while a second camera showed the winner's excited face as she called out her purchases. 'I'll take the dinette set for five-ninety-nine, and the matching sideboard for three-fifty.' There was always a couple of hundred dollars left over, and invariably the winner would have to choose the white, ceramic greyhounds. An had always wanted one of those greyhounds. She'd yet to find one at a store. It was the kind of thoughtful gift Jill would've found for her if she'd had the strength to get out of bed (not that they had a lot of money; Jill's disability pay from the hospital barely helped with her part of the mortgage).

Bruce knocked on the door as he entered the interrogation room. He held a folder in his hand; the crime-scene photos. He put the folder on the table and slid it toward An as a twelve-year-old boy in a suit walked in behind him.

Well, the public defender couldn't have actually been twelve, but he looked it. When he walked across the room, his shoes squeaked. She noticed that his hair was wet at the crown where he'd combed down a cowlick. The sleeve of his suit still had the manufacturer's label sewn on to the cuff.

'I'm Max Jergens,' he said, and An nearly laughed, thinking the name would be more fitting for a well-endowed porn star. She couldn't help it, her eyes went directly to his crotch. Jergens noticed, of course. His lip curled up in a smile.

An tried to sound professional, and to not look at his crotch, when she told him, 'I'm Detective An Albada. We have some questions for your client in connection with the death of one of his co-workers, Sandra Burke.'

He put his briefcase on the table, opened the locks, took out a legal pad, closed the briefcase, put it on the floor, sat down at the table, took a pen out of his breast pocket, took the cap off the pen and put it on the opposite end, then wrote down the word, 'Anabada.'

Martin said helpfully, 'I made the same mistake myself,' as he took the pen from his lawyer, crossed through the word and wrote in a flourishing script much like a teenage girl's, 'Detective Anther Albada.' He even put a circle instead of a dot over the 'i'.

Bruce chuckled behind An. She didn't have to turn around to know that he had his arms crossed over his chest and was staring down his nose at Martin.

Jergens asked, 'What evidence do you have against my client?'

Martin began, 'It's silly, really—' but An cut him off with a 'Was he talking to you?' look.

She said, 'We found blood on Mr Reed's car, his own mixed with that of the victim. We have conclusive evidence that it was Mr Reed's car that ran over Ms. Burke.'

Martin's face turned a whiter shade of pale. 'I cut my hands,' he explained. 'The bumper was hanging off the front of my car. My hands got cut.' He held up his palms and she saw the criss-cross of razor-thin lines. They had taken photographs of the wounds when they were booking him, and An had thought then as she thought now that had Sandra Burke been felled by a mortal paper cut, this would have been an open and shut case.

Jergens asked, 'Where was her body found?'

'Less than half a mile from Mr Reed's place of employment – the same route he takes home every day.'

Jergens seemed surprised. 'Is that so?'

'We believe he took his mother home, then went in search of the woman who had humiliated him two days before.' An watched Martin as she laid out the scenario. He didn't look like someone who would fester with hatred, but then again, she was a grown woman who had carried on an eight-year relationship with an imaginary friend, so who could tell?

Jergens asked, 'Does he have an alibi?'

'No.'

'Ouch!' Jergens chortled. He looked down at his legal pad where he was tracing An's name with his pen. When he saw her watching, he gave her a wink and turned one of the circles into a heart.

'Are you narcoleptic?' Martin asked his lawyer.

Jergens shook his head sadly. 'Don't I wish.'

An opened the folder Bruce had given her, keeping it tilted so that Martin and his boy lawyer could not see the contents. The pictures were stark, violent. Sandy had not just been hit by a car. Her body showed extensive bruising where she had been beaten repeatedly with a blunt object. On the scene, the coroner had guessed maybe a piece of wood or something with a square end. When An had opened the trunk of Martin's Camry and seen the crushed corner of his briefcase, she had added the case to the list of possible murder weapons.

The coroner easily read the scene: the car had been used to knock down the victim. The subsequent beating was what had killed the woman. Then, the killer had gotten back into his car and ran over her head. Then her torso. Then her head again.

An had to admit, if only to herself, that she was having trouble feeling sympathy for the victim. Sandra Burke had two children who were being raised by the State. She had a history of drug and alcohol abuse. She had been arrested once for intimidating one of her elderly neighbors into giving her ten dollars for cigarettes.

All of this together was nothing spectacularly bad in the scheme of things – this was certainly not the first case An had seen where an alcoholic, bad mother had been brutally murdered – but there was one particular thing about Sandra Burke that really grated An's nerves: she was a hideous housekeeper. She'd left plates in the sink so long that the food had started to grow mold. How hard was it to put them in the dishwasher? And would it have killed the woman to occasionally vacuum the rug in the front hall? For the love of God, the vacuum was right there in the hall closet.

'Excuse me?' Martin said.

An realized she had gone silent too long. She cleared her throat, trying to block out the image of the dirty dishes, to think of Sandra Burke as a human being instead of a grossly untidy person. 'Mr Reed, have you ever hit a woman?'

He bristled. 'Of course not. Men are stronger than women. It's an unfair advantage.'

Bruce chuckled. 'Have to be alone with them before you can hit them, right, Marty? Was that what it was all about?' He slammed his hands on the table, raising his voice. 'Tell us what happened, Martin! Tell us the truth!' He leaned closer. 'You came on to Susan and she told you to go fuck yourself! Isn't that right?'

Martin and An exchanged a look. His voice was mild when he corrected, 'It's Sandy, actually.'

Jergens scratched through the word 'Susan' on his pad and wrote 'Sandee'.

An felt a headache working its way up from the back of her neck and into the base of her brain. She asked, 'Mr Reed, where did you go last night after you dropped off your mother?'

'I just drove around,' he mumbled.

'Speak up,' Bruce chided.

'I said I just drove around,' Martin insisted. 'This is really crazy. Honestly, why would I hurt Sandy?'

An kicked Bruce's foot with her own, indicating that he should go back to glowering with his back against the wall. She told Martin, 'Your co-workers claim Sandy taunted you quite a bit.'

'No, she didn't,' Martin countered. 'Well, I mean, not in a disrespectful way. Not to be cruel, I mean. Well, maybe it was a bit cruel, but she didn't mean to hurt—'

'Two days ago, she went on the loudspeaker

and called you "teeny weenie" then Super Glued a twelve-inch vibrating rubber dildo to your desk.'

Martin cleared his throat. 'She liked her pranks.'

'Apparently.'

'And Sandy knows that Super Glue can be easily removed with GlooperGone. It's one of Southern's best-selling products.' He shook his head. 'She started out on the Glooper line, for goodness' sakes.'

An tried not to imagine Martin gripping a twelve-inch vibrating dildo as he lubed it with solvent and scraped it from his desk. 'Some of the women we talked to said that you listen to them while they are urinating in the toilet.'

Jergens' lip curled in disgust. 'Seriously, dude?'

Martin explained, 'My office is right outside the toilets. I wasn't listening. I didn't have a choice.'

'Yeah, right.' Jergens went back to his doodling. An could see he had drawn a hangman's gallows with a figure resembling Humpty Dumpty hanging from the noose.

An suggested, 'Mr Reed, you can clear this up if you just tell us where you were last night.'

'I told you I drove around. I was home by

eight – there was a television program I wanted to watch.'

Jergens perked up. 'What'd you watch?'

Martin looked down, his face reddening. He mumbled something unintelligible.

An, Bruce and Jergens all asked, 'What?' at the same time.

Martin held his head up high, squared his shoulders. '*Dancing With the Stars*.'

Jergens shot Bruce a look, and both men chuckled. 'Did you watch it with your mommy?'

An stared at the lawyer, for some reason feeling protective of the suspect.

Martin answered, 'Yes, I watched it with my mother.' An could tell that he was struggling to hold on to a sliver of his dignity.

She asked, 'Did you watch it all the way through?'

Martin nodded. 'Mother went to bed when Mr T was doing the rumba, and as I am a lifelong A-Team fan, I wanted to see what would happen.' He added, 'There's nothing feminine about wanting to watch people dance. Mr T is very light on his feet. He's an amazing athlete. Lots of athletes take dancing lessons. It makes them more nimble.'

An sighed again, sitting back in the chair. Sandra Burke had been murdered around eight-fifteen, which, if An was remembering correctly, was around the same time one of the *Dancing With the Stars* judges had commented that, in fact, many athletes were nimble dancers.

Martin could not stop defending his masculinity. 'There is nothing wrong with having a wide variety of interests. I am interested in many things. Very many interesting things.'

'Books?'

Martin smiled – a genuine smile. 'I love to read.'

'What subjects are you most interested in?'

'Well, murder mysteries. Science fiction, but more about social issues than space ships.' He stared down as his hands, almost bashful. 'I'm particularly fond of Kathy Reichs. Her main character is very . . . alluring. She gets to the bottom of things, like, you know . . . you.'

An felt her face flush. She never missed an episode of *Bones*. Was he comparing her to Tempe Brennan?

Bruce wasn't buying it. 'Come on, Reed. Dr Brennan is a forensic anthropologist.'

'He's right, man,' Jergens agreed, seeming to

forget that Martin was his client. 'Andi is a detective.'

'Anther,' Martin corrected. 'Detective Anther Albada.' He kept his eyes on An as he pressed a doughy finger to the legal pad where he had written her name. 'Anther.'

An had started to chew her cuticle again. She made herself stop. Things had gotten off track, and she could not for the life of her figure out how. She asked Martin, 'Do you read true crime?'

'Definitely. But only Ann Rule – not the trashy stuff. Oh, and I never look at the pictures.'

An opened the folder so Martin could see the photos. 'Pictures like these?' she asked, flipping picture after picture around, showing him Sandra Burke splayed naked, her body creased where again and again the car had backed up and driven over her. 'We found parts of her teeth in your back right tire.'

Martin opened his mouth and vomited all over the table.

What Martin Really Did That Night, or All That Glitters is to Goad

Martin often said that he did not have a racist bone in his body. He had supported Barack Obama, or at least he had told people that he did (Martin's life was run by strong women; he was not one to embrace change). His closest co-worker was black. He occasionally listened to rap music and enjoyed the comedy of Chris Rock. He was, in short, a man who did not normally see black and white. When he looked at a person, he saw a person, not a skin color.

Even with these sterling credentials, Martin could not help but notice that he was the only white man in the holding tank at the Atlanta jail. Neither had the color discrepancy gone unnoticed by his fellow prisoners. When he had first entered the cell, someone had noticed

Martin's short-sleeved dress shirt and his clip-on tie and said, 'Look, a Republican.'

He could not believe that they were holding him on such flimsy evidence. Sure, his blood was mixed in with Sandy's . . . stuff . . . but that didn't mean anything. Or did it? One need only read a good Patricia Cornwell to know that blood did not come with a time-and-date stamp. Scientifically, there was no way to prove that Martin had touched the bumper the day after the incident. What a mess!

He held his breath as the odor of fresh feces filled the air. There were two toilets, both of them out in the open for the world to see. A large, bald man was sitting reading a magazine, doing his business as if this was just another day in his life. Martin had dealt with being around toilets most of his adult life and had tucked himself into the far corner when he had first entered the cell, but the odor seemed to bounce off the walls and envelop him. Sitting on the floor with his knees to his chest, all Martin could think about was this was how the system turned you into an animal. How long would it take before Nature won out and he was forced to relieve himself in front of complete strangers? How long before his dignity was completely removed and he was spitting on the floor and scratching himself alongside the other screws? Or was it fishes? Martin had still not mastered the lingo.

Oh, if only his one phone call had been made to his father instead of his useless mother. She hadn't answered the phone. The answering machine had whirred, Evie's blunt voice saying to leave a message. He knew she was home—Evie could not drive herself anywhere because of her cataracts – just as he knew that she was aware that Martin was sitting – no, rotting! – in jail.

His father would not have left his only son among these monsters. His father would have . . . oh, who was he kidding? Marty Reed has been just as useless in life as he was in death. An accountant, like his son would grow up to be, Marty had worked in indexing and actuarials for a large law firm downtown. His mother had called it 'the accident' right up until the insurance company had asserted that no matter how many times she insisted, the cause of Martin Harrison Reed Senior's death had been officially ruled a suicide.

This was how it had happened: Marty had enjoyed a nice lunch of ham salad with a devilled egg. He had written a note on the back of an index card and taken off his glasses. He left both of these on his desk. The sight of Marty fumbling blindly through the office, bumping into chairs and walls (he was legally blind without his glasses) as he made his way toward the hallway, did not strike anyone as unusual at the time. He had the remnants of his sack lunch in his hand as he felt his way toward the trash chute. Someone reported hearing a giggle as the door squeaked open, though that would have been the last noise he made. Marty didn't even scream as he careened down the chute, landing thirty-eight floors down beside his wadded up lunch sack.

It wasn't until several hours later when the driver of the garbage truck found the body that someone actually read the note: 'Please give my glasses to the Ancient Arabic Order of the Nobles of the Mystic Shrine.'

'That's nice,' Martin's mother had said, though she had been furious to learn that the Shriners did not allow women to attend their meetings. Martin had always assumed that explained the giggle. His father had finally managed to get the last word.

'Hooty-hoo!' someone heckled. There were

whistles and a few catcalls. Martin craned to see around the legs of the men standing in front of the cell bars. He saw a tennis shoe . . . a calf . . .

'Shut up, you cocksuckers,' An told the men who were reaching toward her. 'Back the fuck off before I Tase every one of you.'

Martin scrambled to stand, his heart thumping at the sound of her voice. The crowd parted and he walked forward, feeling the curious, if not outright envious, stares of his fellow cellies.

An nodded to the policeman beside her and he opened the cell door.

'This way,' she said, walking down the hallway.

Martin stumbled over his own feet as he tried to keep up with her. 'It was awful in there,' he said. 'You don't know what it does to a man. They're animals. I feel so—'

'You were in there for less than thirty minutes,' she told him, punching a code into the keypad by the door.

'Really?' he asked, surprised that it hadn't been at least an hour. 'It felt like an eternity. Thank you so much for . . .' Martin's brain caught up with the moment. 'Hey, where are you taking me?'

'I'm letting you out on your own recognizance.'

'What about the blood? What about my fingerprints?'

'Are you trying to talk me out of this?'

'I just . . . I don't want you to get into trouble,' he said, the truth coming out. His mind flashed on the image of An in the interrogation room. Was that concern he had seen on her face as he threw up all over the table? It wasn't revulsion – Martin had seen revulsion in enough women by now to know what that looked like.

She asked, 'Why would I get in trouble?'

'For letting me out,' he said. 'I mean, this is a lot of circumstantial evidence we're talking about.'

She stared at him. He saw that one of her eyelids drooped more than the other. The circles under her eyes were darker in the fluorescent light of the corridor. He wanted to hold her in his arms. He wanted to kiss the droopiness away. Or kiss the droopiness in, because it seemed like it would be easier to make an eyelid droop more by pressing into it than it would be to remove the droopiness; it was just simple physics.

'You need a better lawyer than the one you've got.'

'Max seems like a nice guy.' He had actually offered Martin some good advice about making sure to align himself with the whites as soon as he got into the cells. Had there been any white people, he would have certainly done so.

'I'm letting you go because forensic tests showed that Sandy's blood on the bumper dried before yours did.'

'You can tell that?'

'Yes,' she told him, sounding tired. 'We can tell that.'

Martin scratched his chin, wondering if he would ever be able to trust Kay Scarpetta again.

'Your car is in the impound lot. Keep your nose clean,' An warned him. 'You're still our main suspect in this case.'

'Yes, I can see why.'

'You also need to tell me what you were doing between the time you dropped off your mother and the time you came home.'

Martin pressed his lips together.

'Mr Reed—'

'I promise you that I would never hurt Sandy. She teased me sometimes, but I know that she cared about me. Sometimes, when people pick on you, it's because, for them, that's the only way they can show affection.' Martin shrugged. 'If you look at it that way, Sandy and I were actually friends.'

An stared at him. She sighed a deep raspy sigh of exhaustion. Martin thought of all the things he would do if he had her all to himself: stroke her hair, rub her feet, change her lightbulbs (even if there were spiders!). He would learn to cook for her. The art of lovemaking would come easily to him, the way that macramé and model ship-building had come to him in the ninth grade. And didn't his mother still have some of his ships on the top of the kitchen cabinets? Evie wouldn't still be displaying them after all of these years if she didn't think they were good!

'Mr Reed?'

She had been talking and he'd missed it. 'Yes?'

My love . . .

'Leave.'

He saw that she was holding the door open for him. A man sat behind a cage with the envelope containing Martin's personal effects. He turned around to thank Anther – really to get one more look at her – only to see the door slam in his face.

The man in the cage started speaking as Martin approached. 'Count your money, check your belongings and sign here.'

Martin followed each step, counting down to the last penny, checking his wallet to make sure an unclaimed scratch-off ticket was still there. 'Thank you,' he told the man, but apparently the fish were just as impolite as the screws. Or was it the screws who controlled the fish? And why did they call them fish? Perhaps because they were swimming against the tide instead of schooling along with the rest of society?

Martin considered this as he walked through the packed lobby of the jail. There was row after row of vinyl seats, enough to handle at least five hundred people, he guessed. Families were waiting in huddled groups. Grandparents sat alone. Such sadness.

There was a taxi-stand outside the jail entrance. Martin got into the first one, which smelled vaguely of vomit. Or maybe he just became aware of his own smell in the cramped quarters. The driver seemed none too pleased. He rolled down all the windows as he merged on to the interstate. Martin's hair flapped wildly around his face, stinging his cheeks, but he did not care. He stared out the window at the downtown skyline as the driver jumped on I-20, then I-285. It wasn't until they passed Atlanta Airport that Martin realized the driver was taking the longest route possible.

Well, Martin thought. *If the driver assumed he was getting a tip, he was dead wrong.*

They pulled up in front of the Reed house exactly fifty-two minutes later. Martin was barely able to pay the price on the meter. The driver made it clear this was unacceptable. He backed the cab over a row of Evie's plants as he zoomed down the driveway. The man probably thought he was punishing Martin, but the truth was that Martin was so mad at his mother for not coming to his aid that he did not care how many flowers were sacrificed.

'What the hell are you doing home?' Evie demanded. She stood in the open doorway of the house, bathrobe hanging open. 'You're supposed to be in prison.'

'Jail,' he corrected. 'Prison is where you go when you're convicted.'

'Thank you for the lesson, Mr fucking Smarty-Pants.'

Martin walked up the front steps and went

into the house. He stopped at the hall mirror, noting how much he had aged since this morning. Living life on the wrong side of the tracks would do that to you.

'Norton Shaw called. He says you're fired.'

'What?'

'He said to get your things after work and leave your keys in his office. I hope you don't think you're going to stay here freeloading off me. I'm an old woman. I have to look out for myself.'

'Why would they fire me?'

'I dunno, Martin. Lemme go out on a limb here and say it's because you murdered one of your God damn co-workers.'

Martin felt his jaw ache from grinding his teeth. 'I need to borrow your car.'

'Why, is there someone else you want to kill?'

He closed his eyes and slowly counted to ten. 'One . . . two . . . three . . .'

'I always thought you might be autistic,' his mother muttered as she headed into the kitchen. 'I wonder if that could be part of your defense.'

Martin opened his eyes. His job! His liveli-hood! His co-workers were the only friends he had. What would he do without this social outlet? Where would he go for the camaraderie, the connection to the outside world? He studied himself in the hall mirror. The hardness in his eyes was new. Was this the man that An had seen, this alternative Martin who viewed the world as a desperate and dastardly place?

Evie tossed the keys at Martin. He tried to catch them as they bounced off his face. 'Fill it up with gas before you bring it back.'

Martin leaned down to pick up the keys. 'It should have a full tank.'

'I had to get some things at the store. I'm an old woman with a fucking criminal for a son. Who knew how long you'd be in the pokey?'

Martin tried not to think about his mother driving. Her cataracts had robbed her of all peripheral vision. She had side-swiped the mailbox last week with the riding lawnmower.

He glanced at his watch. Southern Toilet Supply would be closed by now. 'I'm going to work to clean out my desk,' he told her, sadness enveloping him. How could he be fired? Why would Norton Shaw do this to him? Martin had not been convicted of a crime. He liked Sandy. Why on earth would he kill her? *How* on earth could he kill her? He didn't even like killing insects.

Evie narrowed her eyes at him. 'If you were really innocent, you'd threaten Southern with a lawsuit for firing you without cause.'

'I am innocent!' he screamed. 'Mother, you know I was home last night.'

She gave her Cheshire Cat grin. They both knew that this was not entirely the truth.

It seemed fitting that Martin drove his mother's car to Southern Toilet Supply. He felt as if he was living inside a Janet Evanovich novel, so it was only natural that, like Stephanie Plum, he was stuck behind the wheel of an elderly relative's powder blue Cadillac. This was no farcical murder mystery, though. This was real life. As if to put a fine point on it, Martin slowed the car at the sight of the police tape marking the scene of Sandy's death.

Poor Sandy. Poor broken Sandy. Sure, she had teased him, but that didn't mean that she deserved to die. Even Evie had said as much. 'What a corker!' she had exclaimed when Martin told her about the fiasco with the glued sex instrument. (Evie had asked about the piece of rubber that the GlooperGone had mysteriously melted into his thumb. Even two weeks later, the faded purple line was still there.)

The car behind him beeped its horn and Martin pressed the accelerator, pulling away from the scene of the crime. He still kept the speedometer well under the limit as he drove to Southern, mindful that An had warned him to keep his nose clean. He thought the warning was very kind of her, but then An seemed like a kind person. He still could not get over the caring look she had given him in the interrogation room just before she'd jumped out of her chair to get away from the splatter of vomit that flooded the table. He hoped that she had copies of those photos he'd ruined. She would need them for her case.

The car behind him swerved into the oncoming lane of traffic, horn blaring as it darted in front of the Cadillac.

'Oh, dear,' Martin muttered, jerking the steering wheel, trying to get out of the way. The wheels bumped on to the shoulder of the road and he turned sharply into the parking lot of a strip mall, hands gripping the wheel, foot slamming on to the brake. The car shuddered to a stop. Martin looked up in time to see a neon sign blinking to life in the afternoon dusk.

Madam Glitter's. If Martin were really in a novel, this would be a prime example of foreshadowing. Or was it aftershadowing? Because, in fact, the thing had already happened.

The truth was that Martin had, in fact, taken his mother to get her trowel from the Peony Club's storage facility, which was directly across the street from the strip mall wherein Madam Glitter's was housed. Martin had sat in his mother's Cadillac (she refused to be seen in the 'twat-mobile'), watching the sign glow in the evening light. 'Stressed? Tired out? Need a lift?' the letters had asked. 'Professional Massage at Reasonable Prices! Walk-ins welcome!'

Martin had never had a massage, and the truth was that ever since he'd spent three hours scraping the last remnants of the vibrating dildo off his desk, his back was killing him. There was a kink in his neck and a knot just under his shoulder blade that felt as if a hot knife was jabbing between his ribs every time he moved his right arm. What was massage for if not that very thing?

He had thought about the massage the entire

drive back to the house, drowning out Evie's complaints about 'that bitch who runs the gardening club like she's the head Nazi at Dachau.'

This is what he imagined: an earthy young woman with a ring in her nose and bare feet would meet him at the front door. Maybe there would be some nice hot tea and cookies. Chimes would tinkle, perhaps the burbling of a small fountain would fill the air. Was there such a thing as a healing touch? Martin had read about a study in one of his magazines where rabbits were being used to test cholesterol medication. One of the rabbit groups showed amazing results, and it was later learned that the keeper of the group had been stroking their backs when she fed them. Could the same thing happen for Martin? Could the loving strokes of another human being change some intrinsic part of him into a happy being?

'I'll be back later,' Martin had told his mother, pulling away from the curb in front of the house as soon as Evie was out of the car.

'What the fuck—' she said, just before the forward motion jerked the car door closed.

As he drove, Martin felt himself relax just thinking about the massage. He even sped, pushing the Cadillac five miles over the posted speed limit. He was picturing this new, reckless side of himself. What would Unique say tomorrow when he managed to slip into the conversation that he had gotten a massage? Would he be some kind of metrosexual because of this? Would he start using scented shaving cream for his weekly shave? Would he get pedicures like Unique? Ha! Wouldn't she think that was funny? Wouldn't she be jealous!

He pulled up in front of Madam Glitter's and parked right outside the front door. As soon as he got out of the car, his feelings of elation started to leave him. Heavy drapes covered the windows. The front door had a large handicap sticker on it, the words, 'We specialize in special needs' underneath. Worse, there was a fast-food restaurant next door, so that when Martin entered Madam Glitter's, he was overwhelmed by the scent of fried chicken.

'You want a massage?' the woman behind the desk demanded. She was large, possibly one of the largest people he had ever seen (and that was saying a lot – there were some beefy women on Evie's side of the family).

'I was . . . uh . . .' Martin felt his feet start to move backward.

'Fifty dollars. I don't take credit cards.' The woman nodded toward a closed door. 'Go in there, take off your clothes and I'll be there in a second.'

Martin stood where he was, frozen in place.

'Move,' she barked, so Martin did.

The chicken smell was even more over-powering in the small massage room. There was a table in the center with a single hand towel at the place where Martin supposed his lower half would rest. He unclipped his tie and hung it on a hook jutting out of the wall. His hands shook as he unbuttoned his dress shirt, and he felt silly for it, because, after all, this was a therapeutic massage, not a *date*, for goodness' sake.

Still, how long had it been since he had been naked in front of a woman? He tried to think back. There had been a girl in high school, a sweet young lady who wore a back brace to correct her scoliosis. Wendy. Martin smiled at the thought of her, the way her curved spine had felt against his palm. If only she hadn't transferred to a magnet school for smart kids in Atlanta. Then there was Marcia, the woman who worked at the convenience store down the street from Martin's house. That had been something of a misunderstanding, though. Unfortunately, Martin had not realized until he was fully naked that Marcia was, in fact, still fully clothed and walking out the door.

The door opened and he grabbed the towel, covering his nakedness.

'I gotta make this fast,' the woman said, picking up his pants off the floor. She pulled out his wallet as she talked. 'My kid's got the 'flu. I thought he was lying to get out of school, but his sister called and said he has a fever.'

Martin watched her count out fifty dollars and return the wallet to his pants. 'I'm sorry to hear that.'

She reached her hand into an open tub of lotion. 'Lie back on the table.'

Martin got on the table, trying to keep the hand towel over his intimate areas.

'You got kids?' she asked, rubbing the lotion into her hands.

Martin's mouth opened to answer just as her hand went under the towel and her fingers wrapped around his member. 'Good Lord!' he yelped.

'Sorry my hands are cold.' She was staring at the wall, a bored look in her eyes as her shoulder jerked back and forth with her hand. 'I tell you what, sometimes I wonder if the government's telling us the truth.'

'Huh-huh.' Martin was panting so hard he could barely speak.

'I mean, lookit this 'flu thing that's going around.' Jerk, jerk, jerk. 'Everybody I know who gets it, they're, like, laid up for a week, then they get a little better, but two months later, they're still feeling rundown.'

Martin gripped the sides of the table, trying not to fall off.

'Can you really trust the CDC? Aren't they supposed to be tracking this shit?'

'Huh-huh-huh . . .'

'And the FDA – one minute they're telling us drugs are safe, the next minute they're taking them off the shelves.'

'Oh-oh-oh . . .'

'It's like we can't trust a thing they tell us anymore.'

Martin closed his eyes, trying to block out the sight of the fat on the back of Madam Glitter's arm swaying as her hand moved. He squeezed his eyes shut even tighter, trying to think about Angelina Jolie, Rebecca Romijn . . . it wasn't until his mind conjured the image of Diane Sawyer in a lilac cashmere sweater that he felt himself starting to let go.

It was the dulcet tones of Diane he heard instead of Madam Glitter's harsh voice when she asked, 'You want me to squeeze your balls?'

'Gah! Gah! Gah!' He came like an oscillating lawn sprinkler with a kink in the hose.

Madam Glitter wiped her hands on the towel. 'Sorry to rush you, but I need to get back to my kid.'

Martin stared up at the ceiling, still panting. There was a brown water stain directly over the table. How had he not noticed that before?

She patted his thigh. 'Come on, sport. Up you go.'

Martin struggled to sit up. The vinyl squeaked as he moved. He was sweating. His chest was still heaving.

The last thing she had said to him as she rushed him out the door was, 'You really should have that mole looked at.'

And this was what Martin was supposed to tell Anther, that he had been getting his member massaged while Sandy was being killed? What kind of alibi was that? What kind of person paid for sex? He would rather be convicted as a murderer than have his mother find out what he had done. Did she have any inkling as to where Martin had really been? Evie was in bed when he returned from the massage parlor. Fortunately, *Dancing With the Stars* was on his TiVo season pass manager. He had watched Mr T doing the rumba with Joan Crawford and thought, *Is this what my life has come to? I actually paid a mother of two for sex?* Or was it really sex? Did a handjob count as intercourse? Martin assumed you had to enter someone – or was that a different 'inter' that they were talking about? Internal? He scowled. That didn't sound sexy at all.

Martin put the Cadillac into reverse and drove away from the scene of his real crime. The parking gate was up at Southern Toilet Supply, which was a direct violation of company rules. Of course, Martin didn't belong to the company anymore, so he shouldn't have given a fig. The problem was that he did give a fig. Anyone could break into this place. Maybe these new people who hadn't had to pick 2300 from the machinery didn't appreciate what mayhem vandals could bring to a place like this, but Martin knew first hand.

He pulled the Cadillac into its usual space, surprised to see that the only other car in the lot belonged to Unique. She certainly wasn't one to work extra hours, but maybe her conscience had won her over. Martin had every intention of completing his receivables from the workday he had missed. He may have been fired, but that was certainly no reason to shirk his responsibilities.

Martin took out his keys as he approached the entrance, but found that the door was already unlocked. He didn't bother to turn on the lights as he made his way to the office. There was no point, really. He knew everything from memory – the way the machinery was positioned, the way the shelving was stacked. For half of his life, this had been Martin's home, the place where he had felt valuable, needed. And now it was all gone – lost like a sock in the dryer, never to be seen again.

'Whatchu doin' here, Fool?' Unique's hands moved quickly as she shoved office supplies into her purse.

'I've been fired.'

'Uh-huh,' she mumbled, cramming her stapler into a side pocket. 'Norton said he was looking for a reason to get rid of you.'

'Get rid of me?' Martin echoed. That couldn't be right. Norton Shaw had given him an 'adequate' on his yearly review. You didn't call someone adequate if you were trying to get rid of them.

'Whatchu doin' outta jail anyway?' she asked. 'I thought you'd be in the electric chair by now.'

'It's lethal injection,' Martin corrected. 'Are you stealing office supplies?'

'Getting out while the getting's good,' she told him, trying to jam a ream of paper into her bag. 'Unique can read the writing on the wall.'

Martin cringed. She only ever spoke of herself in the third person when she felt threatened. He could still remember the first time he'd heard her do it. Martin had suggested that it was only fair that she clean the women's room as he was expected to clean up after the men. 'Unique don't clean toilets!' she had screeched.

He tried, 'Unique—'

'I don't need no trouble with the po-lice,' she told him. 'No way is Unique sticking around with the po-lice asking questions.'

'What kinds of questions?'

'I might have bought some clothes at the mall that one time that I didn't exactly pay for.'

Martin was outraged. 'You *stole*?'

She indicated her bright purple silk pantsuit. 'You think I can dress like this on what y'all pay me?'

Actually, he did.

'I got a look to uphold,' she told him, pushing Martin out of the way as she walked around to his desk. 'You don't go messing with a lady's wardrobe.'

Perhaps it was because of his own recent brush with the law, but Martin felt his outrage quickly turn into fascination. He had worked with this woman for three years without knowing that she was an actual thief. 'Did you get caught?'

'There might be a warrant out there somewhere. You know how it is.'

Had she winked at him? Martin thought she had. 'Yes,' he said. 'Having spent some time in jail myself, I understand.'

She looked at him, her lips pursed. Was that respect in her eyes?

'I fought the fishes,' he told her, trying out his jail-house lingo.

She turned skeptical. 'Fought them on what?'

'Well, you know, jail is very divisive. I had to

hook up with the whites, you see. Immediately, you have to choose a posse.'

'Posse?'

He leaned on the edge of her empty desk. 'Peeps, you might have heard it called.'

She dumped a box full of invoices on the floor and started filling it with Post-it notes from Martin's desk. 'Did you really kill Sandy?'

'Well, I . . .' he fumbled for words. 'She teased me quite harshly.'

Unique stopped filling the box. 'You was mad after the dildo, huh? I saw it in your eyes when that rubber melted into your thumb.' She chuckled. 'I knew there was something more to you, Martin.'

Martin. She had called him Martin. Not Fool. Not Doughboy. Martin.

'She pissed you off, didn't she?'

The only thing he could think to say was, 'Live by the dildo, die by the dildo.'

Unique's eyes widened in shock. 'Did you rape her?'

He shrugged again, thinking this was the most attention she had ever given him. She was actually talking to him like a human being!

'Tell me what happened,' she whispered,

letting him know that it was just between the two of them. 'I promise I won't tell nobody. Just for my own sake, let me know.'

'Well, I—'

'It was all about the sex, wasn't it?'

Martin waved this away with his hand, slightly queasy by the thought of rape, especially having just spent nearly a full half-hour in a cage of savage men. 'I've got a girl who takes care of those needs.'

She gasped. 'You been paying for sex? Seeing prostitutes? Martin, that's what Ted Bundy did!'

Having read *The Stranger Beside Me* five times, Martin was certain her statement was untrue, but he could not find it in himself to burst her bubble, so he said, 'Yes, I'm just like Ted Bundy.'

'Where?' she asked. 'Do you go into Atlanta? Do you make them do nasty things?'

Martin shrugged again, hoping she couldn't see how red-faced he was becoming. 'There's a lady – name'a Glitter. I use her to satiate my needs.'

'To get your anger out, right?' She took a few steps toward him. 'You're a really angry man, ain't you, Pasty?'

'I've got a temper.'

'I heard about you stomping on that briefcase,' she said. 'Is that what you used to kill her?'

He shrugged for maybe the sixtieth time. Was it just him, or was Unique standing closer? He could have reached out and touched her. So he did.

'Oh, baby,' she breathed, as if his touch brought a tingle to her skin. 'Do it again.'

He touched her bare arm, his creamy fingers a stark contrast to her black coffee. Suddenly, both her hands clamped around his head. She yanked him off the desk and crammed his face into her voluminous breasts. Martin couldn't breathe. His feet slid on the tiled floor as he tried to back away from her.

'Come'ere,' she grunted, her long, red finger-nails scraping against his belly as she yanked down his pants. Martin didn't plunge so much as fall into her. She gripped his ass cheeks so hard between her fists that he felt like his butt was being molded into a handle. She certainly used it that way, pushing, pulling, pushing, pulling so that Martin was jackhammering in and out.

He couldn't stop her, and after a few hundred thrusts, he didn't want to stop her. His knees started to go weak. 'Oh-oh-oh!'

'Say it, baby!' she yelled back. 'Say my name!'

'You-knee-kay! You-nee-kay!'

'Say it, Doughboy! Say it louder!'

'You! Nee! Kay! You! Nee! Kay!'

'That's it!' she cried. 'Come on, baby! Fuck Unique! Fuck that baby!' She tugged and yanked and slammed him against her. Martin held on to her shoulders as she jerked his body back and forth.

'Oh! Jesus! Jesus! Jesus!' he cried.

'No, you don't!' she warned him, her hands stopping the motion.

It was too late. He came in torrents, great mighty plumes that would rival Old Faithful in pounds per square inch. His body shook with manly release, his muscles tensing as wave after wave shot through him.

'Nuh-uh,' Unique mumbled. 'No way you're finishing without me, Pillsbury.'

Her hand gripped the back of his head again, pushing his face down between her legs and into the cavernous cleavage of her cleft. Unique was stronger than she looked. Her fingernails dug into the back of his head, pressing Martin's nose against her wetness. He struggled to pull back even as she forced him closer. She started to grind against his face, his nose sliding up and down. Martin fought the urge to sneeze, to choke, to scream for air. He started to hyperventilate again, his brain spinning in his head, and still she pressed his face into her mound like an orange in a juicer, then like cheese in a grater. She was working on pork in a meat grinder when he started to see stars, and not the good kind. His eyelids flickered. Just before he passed out, she finished, or at least he thought she did. Either way, Unique pushed him away from her like he was a dog trying to eat off her plate. Martin fell back, his hands slipping on the tiled floor. His face was so wet that he must have been gleaming. She looked down at him with renewed disgust.

'You ain't all that,' she noted, tugging up her underwear. Her stomach rolled over the top like a muffin over its paper wrapper.

'I was—'

'Shut up, Fool.' She reached into her purse, checking something. 'All right, then,' she mumbled.

Martin had managed to stand but he was so dizzy that he didn't trust himself to reach down and pull up his pants. He put his hand on the desk to steady himself. He should do the gentlemanly thing now, like offer to take her to dinner or maybe suggest a drink. 'Unique, perhaps I could—'

'Pull up your pants, Fool. That weenie of yours ain't nothin' to look at.'

'Oh, sorry.' Martin scrambled to do as he was told.

'Carry that box out to my car,' she ordered. 'And stop looking at me like that. Just 'cause you got a taste of the honey don't mean you can keep buzzing the hive.'

Martin's Unique Problem, or
An's Mary Ever-After

An blew her nose with a tissue even as tears streamed down her face. She should have known better than to start watching *The House of Mirth* while she was on her period. Or maybe An was just sensitive in general. For the life of her, she could not get Martin Reed out of her mind. The way he had compared her to Tempe Brennan . . . the way he had vomited when he'd seen the crime-scene photos (An had always had a soft spot for men with weak stomachs. Her father had suffered from ulcers his entire life). And then there was that look he gave her when she released him from the holding cells – part confused child, part sadistic monster. Would she ever know the real Martin?

An tried to turn her attention back to the movie, mindful that thinking about Martin Reed would never lead her to a good place. The truth was that after Charlie had died, one of the main reasons An had never been able to make a connection with another man was because there was always a little part of her that was scared of being beaten. She hated to admit it (it was the kind of revelation she would only have shared with Jill) but she had decided a long time ago that the perfect man for her would probably be one who could never touch her or get close enough to harm her in any way.

In short, her ideal mate was Jill, but with a penis.

'Ugh,' she groaned. She was too old to change back, and she was pretty certain that she wouldn't be able to scrape the gay flag bumper sticker off her car without removing a chunk of paint in the process.

An tried to concentrate on the movie, holding the box of tissues in her lap. Gillian Anderson's Lily Bart was lying in bed, taking that last fatal dose of laudanum, when An's phone rang.

'Hello?' she sniffed.

'Aw, shit,' Bruce said. 'I knew I shouldn't have let you go home alone. Not with this being Jill's anniversary and all.'

An looked at the paused image of Gillian
Anderson lying in bed. Even close to death, she
was still beautiful. An couldn't help but think
that that's exactly how Jill would have looked if
she had really lived and then really died. Wasn't
laudanum a derivative of opium? Surely they
would have given Jill something for the pain.

'An?'

'I'm okay,' she told him, sniffing again.
'What's up?'

'The security guard from Southern Toilet
Supply just called. He found a dead body in the
bathroom.'

'What?' An gasped, shock making her heart
feel as if it had stopped in her chest. Bruce
explained to her what had happened, but An's
brain could not process his words into anything
that made sense. Even as she got dressed, got into
her car, drove to Southern, flashed her badge at
the police blockade and went into the bathroom,
she still could not quite grasp what Bruce had
told her.

And then she had seen the prone body of
Unique Jones and finally understood.

The woman was lying face down on the floor,
her dress hiked up, legs spread. There was a mop

handle sticking out from between her legs. Blood pooled around her head. Incongruously, the whole bathroom smelled like flowers.

An asked, 'What happened?'

The coroner supplied his theory. 'I'd say she was hit with this,' he said, holding up a clear plastic evidence bag. An saw a wall-mounted bathroom air sanitizer with blood and hair stuck to the crushed tip.

'Came from over there,' Bruce said, pointing to the empty mounting bracket bolted to the wall. 'Lavender scent.'

That explained the smell.

'The blow was fatal,' the coroner explained.

'Was she raped?'

He got down on his knees and craned his neck to look up between the legs. 'Unless he's got a penis the size of a mop handle, I'd say he couldn't perform,' the man noted. 'Typical with sexual offenders. They can't penetrate, so they punish the victim, and *then* they get their sexual release. There's enough jizz here to paint the Capitol dome.'

An shook her head, trying to clear the image that had brought. 'Who found the body?'

'Security guard,' Bruce told her. 'He fell asleep

in the booth.' Bruce pinched his thumb and forefinger together, brought them to his mouth and made a sucking sound. 'Guy likes his weed.' He shrugged; half the cops on the force did, too. 'Anyway, he woke up, saw that Jones' car was still here, went inside and found her like this.'

'Were any other cars in the lot?'

'He pulled the security tape for us,' Bruce said. 'The only other car that came in and out was a powder blue Cadillac.' He paused for effect. 'We ran the plates. The car's registered to Evelyn Reed.'

'Fuck,' An whispered. Martin had promised he would stay out of trouble.

'He seemed agitated that day when he came to work,' Daryl Matheson testified in front of the judge. 'I asked him about the blood on the bumper, and he got really defensive.'

'He was pounding on the briefcase,' Darla Gantry stated, after swearing on the Bible to tell the truth, the whole truth, and nothing but the truth. 'I asked him what he was doing and he told me to mind my own damn' business.'

'Well,' Norton Shaw began, clearly reluctant to be telling this to the jury. 'Martin was always complaining about Unique. I didn't pay much attention to it. He usually complained about a lot of people.'

'He scared me,' Gloria 'Madam Glitter' Koslowski admitted. 'I told him to leave. I didn't want to be alone with him.'

'Unique was always scared of Pasty. He stared at her all the time, looking at her breasts and things.' Renique, Unique's sister, was steely yet composed (she had trouble of her own – it seems the church where she worked had found some accounting irregularities).

Evelyn Reed sobbed, 'I didn't know what to do with him! He was just out of control!'

It must be said that the final nail in Martin Reed's coffin came from his own words. An had found a tape recorder in Unique's purse alongside various purloined office supplies. Cellphone records had shown she'd made several phone calls to the local television stations, offering to sell her story. And what a story it would have been.

On the tape, Unique's voice sounds hurried, almost excited. 'You been paying for sex? Seeing prostitutes? Martin, that's what Ted Bundy did!'

'Yes,' Martin replies, sounding cool, confident. 'I'm just like Ted Bundy.'

Even Max Jergens had looked convinced when An had played the tape in open court. 'No way,' he'd said when the judge had asked if he wanted to cross-examine the witness. 'Dude, did you hear what he said?'

Through it all, Martin sat passively by his lawyer. Or, at least, he seemed to be passive – how could you tell what was going on in Martin Reed's twisted, sick mind?

To her credit, An had tried to find even the slightest bit of evidence in Martin's favor. Each inquiry she made only seemed to dig him deeper into the hole: His fellow employees seemed to think he was a cross between Baby Huey and Charles Manson. Add to that the forensic evidence – Martin's sperm inside Unique, his saliva and sperm on the floor in the office and in his shoe – and there was not much An could do but sit back and wait for the judge's gavel to fall. And fall it did.

'Martin Harrison Reed Junior, I hereby sentence you to death by lethal injection.'

Death! It seemed a bit harsh, but then maybe An had developed a soft spot for Martin over the months of interviewing him. They had spent so many hours together, yet she still felt that she hardly knew him at all. He had even tried to learn Dutch (she hadn't the heart to tell him that her family was actually from Friesland – Dutch was hard enough; Frisian would have probably driven him to suicide). Really, if you didn't look at him or talk to him for very long, he was actually a rather nice guy.

Of course, people had started to notice at work that An was acting differently. Bruce had picked up on it first, noting that she had ironed a shirt or brushed her hair. Working with a bunch of detectives, you'd think one of them would have put together the fact that An only took care of her appearance on the days that she talked with Martin Reed. Then again, the thought of her actually falling for someone who was soon to be a convicted murderer (the case was a slam dunk) was fairly preposterous.

Had she fallen for him? Well – maybe. An tested the waters first, trying to see how it would feel. She sent herself flowers at work (boy, had that caused a stir) and took off early one Friday to get ready for a 'dinner date'. There was teasing and smiles and pats on the back. Part of her was a bit hurt that they seemed to have so easily forgotten Jill, but then Doug, her boss, had called her into his office one day and said, 'You know, I'm glad to see you moving on. Jill would've wanted you to be happy.'

An had felt tears well into her eyes.

'So,' Doug said, a teasing lilt to his voice, 'what's the lucky lady's name?'

'Mary,' she told him, stroking her neck the way that she imagined Jill used to. 'Her name is Mary.'

Martin's Lethal Injection, or Be Steel My Heart

Martin sat at a plastic table in the visitors' lounge, watching his mother get searched for contraband. She kept up a constant stream of chatter as hands patted her down and the wand waved over her body. Apparently, she said something funny, because all the guards laughed. Evelyn Reed was one of the most popular visitors at the prison. Nay, one of the most popular mothers in the country. She had been on every talk show and appeared above the fold on just about every newspaper printed. She was a celebrity of her own making, a star of stage and screen. Even the Ladies' Hospital Auxiliary had begged her to come back.

There was a hush in the nearly packed visitors' lounge as Evie made her way toward Martin. Some women raised their fists in the air to show their solidarity. Others stared in wonderment while still others took advantage of the distraction to pass drugs they had secreted in various cavities.

'Martin,' Evie called, waving her hand as if he couldn't see her. She certainly had a spring in her step these days. She'd started working out with a personal trainer after seeing herself on *Oprah* ('Why didn't you tell me I'd put on weight?'), and between the new exercise regime and her personal chef, she had managed to lose thirty pounds. Add to that the face-lift and the Botox, and you could understand how the 63-year-old-woman before him looked closer to Martin's age than her own.

'Hello, Mother.'

'Oh, why are you always so dire when I come to visit you?' she scoffed, taking a pad and a pen from her Prada bag. 'You're such a downer.'

'I'm on death row.'

'Please,' she grumbled, and he could have sworn she had started using an English accent. 'You should see what these shoes are doing to my bunions.' She held out her leg so he could see the four-inch heel on her Jimmy Choo. 'I wore them on *Regis and Kelly* the other day and by the time

I walked off stage, I was ready to kill somebody.' She had a sparkle in her eye. 'Figuratively speaking, of course.'

'Of course,' Martin said. They both knew what had happened. Martin was no fool – at least he wasn't as big a fool as his mother thought. He had spent a lifetime of reading crime stories and murder mysteries. By simple process of elimination, he had figured it out. There were only two people who could have committed these heinous crimes, and Martin knew *he* hadn't done it.

'Now,' Evie said, writing 'Chapter Twelve' at the top of the page with her bright, gold pen. 'My editor thinks we should talk a bit more about your childhood right after your father died. You're still blaming yourself for that, right?' She seemed hopeful. Martin nodded. 'What about that time I came home and found you in my underwear?'

'That never happened!' he screeched, horrified that the other prisoners might have heard. 'You can't write that!'

A guard appeared instantly. 'Dial it back, Martin.'

He nodded, gripping his hands together under

the table. They were all on his mother's side here. She'd fooled them completely.

'Mother,' Martin began, 'why don't you tell them how you always bought clothes that were too big for me, so that when I went to school I got teased?'

She waved this off with a perfectly manicured hand. 'All mothers do that. Kids grow so fast you can't keep up with them.'

The guard paced back and forth behind Martin, apparently feeling the need to protect Evelyn. Martin kept his mouth shut. He had nothing more to say on the subject. There was no use arguing, because she would only point out that it wasn't her fault that Martin didn't grow. The too-big shoes, the baggy pants, the loose underwear that facilitated wedgies – these would all somehow be turned around on Martin and it would suddenly be his own damn' fault.

'What about men?' she asked, a pleasant lilt to her voice. 'Are you meeting anyone in here?'

Martin just stared at her, listening to the footsteps behind him as the guard paced away.

'Well, I'm trying, Martin. I really am. I come visit you. I talk to you. I try to bring a little happiness in your life . . .' She waited for the guard to pass, leaning over and hissing, 'Listen, you little fucker! If you hate it so bad in here then tell them the truth. Is that what you want to do? How interested do you think your precious detective would be if she knew that you were just a normal everyday putz who couldn't hurt a fly . . . and of course I love you, Martin. I could never hate you. I hate your crimes, but you will always be my son.'

Martin sighed. The guard had come back. He waited for the man to turn again and head in the other direction. 'Tell me how you did it,' he murmured. 'I saw you in bed when I got home from the massage parlor.'

'Massage?' Her eye twitched as her brain sent a message to raise her eyebrow, only to be told that the Botox had paralyzed the nerve. 'Is that what you want to call it, boy-o, a massage?'

'Handjob,' he sighed. His language had gotten coarse in prison, but then you couldn't see a man pull a shiv out of his rectum and stab another man and still say things like, 'Darn, that was a heck of a move, buddy!'

Evie was silent, her lips curved in a tight smile (though, honestly, after the face-lift, everything was tight). The guard walked away and she said, 'Pillows. You saw pillows.'

Martin leaned forward. She seldom talked about this and he wanted to strike while the iron was hot. 'What about when I came home from work?' he asked. 'You said you had a headache.'

'Your father used to fall for that, too,' she cracked. 'I put the car in neutral and rolled it out of the driveway.'

'How did you do it?' Martin whispered, desperate to know. This was where the scenario always got hung up in his mind. He understood that his mother had driven the Cadillac back to Southern Toilet Supply, but he could not for the life of him see anyone, especially Evie, being able to get one over on Unique. She was much too sassy.

Evie sighed, twisting her pen closed. She glanced up at the guard, who was talking to another prisoner. 'It's her own fault for still being there when I drove up. She was loading her car with UrWay.'

Martin 'tsked.' Office supplies were one thing; urine cake quite another.

'I asked her to help me to the bathroom. I'm an old lady, you know. I need help walking sometimes.' She winked on this last part – an unnecessary flourish, Martin felt. 'When we got inside, I "accidentally" dropped a twenty on the floor and pretended not to notice. I headed for the stall, and when she bent down to pick it up, I clobbered her with the sanitizer.'

'Hmm,' Martin said. Death by FreshInator. It seemed appropriate. 'And the mop handle?'

'It had to look sadistic, Martin. The sexual component is what sells.' She added, 'Besides, who would guess in a million years that she'd already had sex with you?'

'Shocked the hell out of me,' he admitted. 'But, what about Sandy? What did she ever do to you?'

'Who do you think wrote "twat" on your car?'

Martin put his hand to his chest. 'That was *Sandy*?'

'No, you idiot, it was me – but it seemed like something she would do.'

She had a point. Sandy could certainly take a prank too far.

'I just . . .' Evie shook her head, her voice catching. 'Martin, I just wanted a better life for us. I wanted you to stand up to people. I thought with the "twat" you might . . .' she shook her head, unable to speak. Martin reached out and held her hand. 'You have no idea how hard it is to raise a child on your own. I feel like I didn't give you things that you needed. Tell me what I did wrong! Tell me how to heal you!'

Martin realized the guard had come back. He let go of her hand.

Evie dabbed under her eyes and smiled at the guard until he left. 'I thought you might grow a pair,' she snapped at Martin. 'I thought it might convince you to actually *do* something with your pathetic, miserable life – but, *noooo*, all you did was complain. "Wah, wah, somebody scratched my car. Poor me. Nobody loves me." If you had confronted Sandy, we wouldn't be here right now.'

'Are you insane? Confronted her for doing something that *you* did?'

'Maybe it would've sent her a message that she couldn't get away with teasing you.' Evie made her voice even lower. 'You never understand, Martin.'

Her attacks were starting to sting. 'What don't I understand?'

'Did it ever occur to you that I was doing you a favor by taking her out? It wasn't easy getting her to meet me. I had to pretend that I had found illegal drugs in your sock drawer.'

'Illegal drugs?'

Evie shrugged. 'She had a problem.'

'Really?' Martin frowned. He'd never pegged Sandy for a drug user.

'That's not the point,' Evie snapped. 'I did it for us, Martin, to give us new lives. When I bashed her in the head, I was bashing her for you. I ran over her three times with your car, Martin. One roll for every decade she humiliated you.'

The math added up, but still Martin shook his head. 'It was never about me. You wanted something bad to happen so you could trot yourself out there as the victim. You couldn't make me gay or give me ALS, so you went out and killed somebody. *Two* somebodys.'

'Martin.'

'The minute I was arrested, you were on the phone with Families and Friends of Violent Criminals.'

'The FFVC has been very kind to me and I don't appreciate your bad-mouthing them,' she quipped. 'And, besides, I could have done something to *you* – did you ever consider that, genius? I could have poisoned you. I could have stabbed you.' She didn't wait for an answer, which was just as well because he didn't have one. 'I could've whacked you over the head and made you retarded or ran over your legs with a lawnmower.' She was clearly exasperated. 'Don't you see, Martin? Can't you understand that this way is better, because we *both* get a second chance out of it?'

Martin threw his hands into the air. 'I give up. I really give up.'

'What is your problem?' she whispered, her voice hoarse. 'Why can't you grasp this basic thing?'

'What basic thing?'

'Is it so wrong to want to be around people? To be cared about? Isn't that why you keep making all those false confessions, so An keeps coming back to interview you?'

Martin crossed his arms over his chest, turning his head to look out the window.

'You've got it pretty sweet in here, Martin. You get to read all day. You work in the warden's office doing the books. The other boys respect you, for once in your life.'

She had a point on that last one, he had to admit. Martin was on death row. People didn't mess with him nearly as much anymore (unsurprisingly, no one wanted to have sex with him in prison, either).

Evie pressed, 'You've carved out a nice little niche for yourself. It's much more than you would have if you were still living with me.'

He shook his head, coming to his senses. 'I think it's pretty obvious who's really benefiting. We have televisions here, Mother. I saw you on *Entertainment Tonight* drinking champagne at George Clooney's villa.'

She smoothed down her skirt, picking an invisible piece of fluff off the cashmere. 'Don't sit there and pretend you're not exploiting your own situation.'

'I'm at least doing some good,' Martin insisted. Some of the crimes he had taken credit for had been unsolved for years. He had read in *People* magazine that the mother of one of his 'victims' had actually said, on her death bed, 'At least now I know.' Was Martin to be blamed for not killing and raping the woman's daughter? Was it *his* fault that he hadn't committed the crime? Was it his fault that he would say anything to keep his beloved Anther coming to see him?

Aye, there's the rub.

'Martin?' Evie snapped her fingers in front of his face. She had packed up her legal pad and pen. 'I have to go. I'm meeting with the producers about your movie.'

Martin scowled. He had not approved of casting Philip Seymour Hoffman in the lead.

'Oh, knock that look off your face. Phil's a lovely boy.' She stood up, pronouncing loudly, 'Now, give your mother a kiss goodbye.'

He puckered up and she put first one cheek, then the other, near enough to his lips to pass for affection.

'I'll see you next month.' She wagged her finger at him. 'And you'd better have some good stories for me. Dark fantasies. Uncontrollable thoughts. Seething hatred. You get the idea.'

Martin rolled his eyes. Bob, one of his favorite guards, came over. Martin held out his hands for cuffing, but the man told him, 'You've got a private visitor.'

'An's here?' Martin felt his heart flutter in his chest. 'She didn't tell me she was coming.'

'They've found another body,' Bob said. 'Thirty-year-old prostitute with a meth habit.'

'Oh, I see,' Martin murmured. He specialized in confessing to prostitute deaths – he'd found early on that this particular type of victim tended to have had very little recent contact with their families, which made it easier for Martin to fabricate a nice backstory. He asked, 'Was this on Madola Road?'

'Abernathy,' Bob provided. 'What were you thinking, man?'

Martin shook his head. 'I just can't help myself, Bob. I get these urges.'

'Why the rope?'

Martin struggled for an explanation. 'My father liked to tie knots.'

Bob sighed at the depravity. Martin knew he was working on his own book deal (it was amazing how many people wanted to be writers). The relationship was not altogether one-sided, though. Bob owned a police scanner and was somewhat of a gossip. Most of the details Martin used in his confessions came from the man.

'Let's go.' Bob took Martin's arm and led him out of the room. As they walked down the corridor toward the private rooms used for interviews between lawyers and their clients – and comely police detectives! – Martin felt his pulse quicken. His breath caught as the door opened and he saw Anther sitting at the table.

She wore a bright yellow dress and her hair was swept up into a sexy bun.

Martin noted her pretty yellow dress and tried to impress her with his Dutch. '*Het meisje draagt een geile jurk!*'

She stared at him, and he felt the skin on his face, wondering if his mother had somehow transferred lipstick on to his cheek without actually touching him.

An said, 'Sit down, Mr Reed.'

He sat.

'We found a body.'

'A prostitute,' Martin supplied. 'A meth addict.'

'She was buried off of—'

'Abernathy Road,' he supplied. 'Have you done something different with your hair?'

She patted the bun self-consciously. 'We found a—'

'Rope,' he said. Why did they always have to go through the motions? 'Tell me about your day.'

'My day?' she echoed, her hand dropping to the table. Martin wanted to reach out and touch her, to caress her gentle hand in his, but the one time he'd tried, An had threatened to Tase him.

Martin spoke openly – prison had made him brazen. 'You know that I am in love with you.'

She gave a sad chuckle. 'Love doesn't pay the rent.'

'*Ik wil de hoer graag betalen,*' he offered, thrilled at the way the Dutch tickled his tongue.

She sighed again. 'Mr Reed—'

'I'd pay your rent every day!' he repeated, this time in English (he had trouble with Dutch tenses). 'Oh, An, you must know that I adore you.'

She colored slightly. There was an awkward moment between them. Then another, then another, so that it was more like an awkward five minutes before she asked, 'Did you read that book I gave you?'

'The Danielle Steel?' Martin had never enjoyed flowery romances, and prison was hardly the place to show your feminine side. 'Well, yes, of course I read it. You know I would do anything you asked me to.'

'She married a prison inmate, you know.'

Martin did not recall that from the plot at all. He gently corrected, 'Actually, Marie-Ange was already married to the Comte de Beauchamp when she suspected him of murdering—'

'No, Mr Reed. Danielle Steel the author. She married a prison inmate. Two, actually.' An shuffled her folders, her eyes avoiding his. 'Danny Zugelder was the first, and then the day after she divorced him, she married William George Toth.'

'Well, that's kind of strange,' Martin said, wondering how the jet-setting Steel would even meet criminals in the first place. 'I bet her mother didn't approve.'

'Maybe she did,' An said, smoothing down the hair at the nape of her neck. 'Maybe her mother said something like, "I just want you to be happy."'

Martin had heard his own mother say the same phrase often enough, but in his experience what she really meant was, 'Do what I fucking say you retarded twat.'

An said, 'I imagine her mother was probably happy to hear that her daughter was in love.'

'I imagine,' Martin answered, though he did not buy it for a minute. He certainly would not mind Evie hooking up with a homicidal maniac, but if it was someone he truly cared about – Anther, for instance – he would certainly have a great deal to say about . . .

Martin cleared his throat, straightened his prison coveralls. 'Married, you say?'

An nodded, flipping through her file folders again. He saw a photo of a decapitated woman in a trench and quickly looked away. (The crime-scene photos were still the worst part of his confessions.)

Martin asked, 'How exactly does that work, I wonder?'

'Well, I suppose that they had the prison chaplain perform the ceremony.'

'I suppose,' Martin agreed, even as he pictured the scene in his mind. An would look lovely in a white dress. Maybe they could get some rice from the kitchen – or better yet, perhaps An could bring some from home. The Latino gang running the kitchen was very stingy, in Martin's opinion. God forbid you should want an extra roll. He imagined asking for rice would cause some kind of riot. Shivs at dawn!

'Martin?'

He let the word hang between them for a few seconds. An seldom used his first name, and Martin tried to savor every time as if it was precious. Because it was. Because, as vile and hateful as his mother could be, she was right

about one thing: the life Martin had in prison
was much better than the one he had when he
was living under her roof. He was a murderer in
here, which actually earned him a modicum of
respect. He had his books. He had a job. And
now . . . was it possible? Was the dream complete
. . . did he actually *have* Anther?

'I'll never get out of here,' Martin reminded
her.

She was looking down, but he could see her
smiling at the thought. 'I know.'

'Even if my sentence is commuted, I'll never—'

'I know,' she repeated, looking up at him.
'You'll never be free. You'll never be able to
touch me or be with me or . . .' her voice trailed
off. 'We can't really get married, Martin. Not
officially.'

'Yes.' He could see that now. An was a
detective and Martin was a convicted triple
murderer (or would be soon. He had another
trial coming up in the spring – the evidence was
not pretty). They were cat and dog, oil and water,
night and day. There were too many things
standing between them; the rice alone was a
logistical nightmare.

An's voice was soft, lilting. 'No one can ever

know about us, Martin. It'll almost be like you're a figment of my imagination.' Her face had colored again, a beautiful shade of red that made the winter-time eczema around her nostrils almost disappear. An asked, 'Do you know what I'm saying, Martin? Do you understand what I mean?'

'*Ja*,' he told her. And it was true. Martin finally understood.

*Read on for an extract from
Karin Slaughter's breathtaking
new thriller . . .*

Fractured

**A broken window. A bloody footprint. Just the
beginning . . .**

When Atlanta housewife Abigail Campano comes home
unexpectedly one afternoon, she walks into a nightmare.
A broken window, a bloody footprint on the stairs and,
most devastating of all, the horrifying sight of her teenage
daughter lying dead on the landing, a man standing over
her with a bloody knife. The struggle which follows
changes Abigail's life forever.

When the local police make a misjudgement which not
only threatens the investigation but places a young girl's
life in danger, the case is handed over to Special Agent
Will Trent of the Criminal Apprehension Team – paired
with detective Faith Mitchell, a woman who resents him
from their first meeting.

But in the relentless heat of a Georgia summer, Will and
Faith realise that they must work together to find the
brutal killer who has targeted one of Atlanta's wealthiest,
most privileged communities – before it's too late . . .

Fractured

PROLOGUE

Abigail Campano sat in her car parked on the street outside her own house. She was looking up at the mansion they had remodeled almost ten years ago. The house was huge – too much space for three people, especially since one of them, God willing, would be going off to college in less than a year. What would she do with herself once her daughter was busy starting a new life of her own? It would be Abigail and Paul again, just like before Emma was born.

The thought made her stomach clench.

Paul's voice crackled through the car speakers as he came back on the telephone. 'Babe, listen—' he began, but her mind was already wandering as she stared up at the house. When had her life gotten so small? When had the most pressing questions of her day turned into concerns about other people, other things: Were Paul's shirts ready at the tailor? Did Emma have volleyball practice tonight? Did the decorator order the new desk for the office? Did somebody remember to let out the dog or was she going to spend the next twenty minutes wiping up two gallons of pee off the kitchen floor?

Abigail swallowed, her throat tightening.

'I don't think you're listening to me,' Paul said.

'I'm listening.' She turned off the car. There was a click, then through the magic of technology, Paul's voice transferred from the car speakers to the cell phone. Abigail pushed open the door, tossing her keys into her purse. She cradled the phone to her ear as she checked the mailbox. Electric bill, Amex, Emma's school fees . . .

Paul paused for a breath and she took that as her cue.

'If she doesn't mean anything to you, why did you give her a car? Why did you take her to a place where you knew my friends might show up?' Abigail said the words as she walked up the driveway but she didn't feel them deep in her gut like she had the first few times this had happened. Her only question then had been, 'Why am I not enough?'

Now, her only question was, 'Why are you such a needy bastard?'

'I just needed a break,' he told her, another old standard.

She dug her hand into her purse for her keys as she climbed the porch stairs. She had left the club because of him, skipped her weekly massage and lunch with her closest friends because she was mortified that they had all seen Paul out with some bottle-blonde twenty-year-old he'd had the gall to take to their favorite restaurant. She didn't know if she would ever be able to show her face there again.

Abigail said, 'I'd like a break, too, Paul. How would you like it if I took a break? How would you like it if you were talking to your friends one day and you knew something was going on, and you had to practically beg them to tell you what was wrong before they finally told you that they saw *me* with another man?'

'I'd find out his fucking name and I'd go to his house and I'd kill him.'

Why did part of her always feel flattered when he said things like that? As the mother of a teenage girl, she had trained herself to look for the positive aspects of even the most savage remarks, but this was ridiculous. Besides, Paul's knees were so bad that he could barely take the garbage down to the curb on trash day. The biggest shock in all of this should have been that he could still find a twenty-year-old to screw him.

Abigail slid her key into the old metal lock on the front door. The hinges squeaked like in a horror movie.

The door was already open.

'Wait a minute,' she said, as if interrupting, though Paul hadn't been talking. 'The front door is open.'

'What?'

He hadn't been listening to her, either. 'I said the front door is already open,' she repeated, pushing it open wider.

'Aw, Jesus. School's only been back for three weeks and she's already skipping again?'

'Maybe the cleaners—' She stopped, her foot crunching glass. Abigail looked down, feeling a sharp, cold panic building somewhere at the base of her spine. 'There's glass all over the floor. I just stepped in it.'

Paul said something she didn't hear.

'Okay,' Abigail answered, automatic. She turned around. One of the tall side windows by the front door was broken. Her mind flashed on a hand reaching in, unlatching the bolt, opening the door.

She shook her head. In broad daylight? In this neighborhood? They couldn't have more than three people over at a time without the batty old woman across the street calling to complain about the noise.

'Abby?'

She was in some kind of bubble, her hearing muffled. She told her husband, 'I think someone broke in.'

Paul barked, 'Get out of the house! They could still be there!'

She dropped the mail onto the hall table, catching her reflection in the mirror. She had been playing tennis for the last two hours. Her hair was still damp, stray wisps plastered to the back of her neck where her ponytail was starting to come loose. The house was cool, but she was sweating.

'Abby?' Paul yelled. 'Get out right now. I'm calling the police on the other line.'

She turned, mouth open to say something – what? – when she saw the bloody footprint on the floor.

'Emma,' she whispered, dropping the phone as she bolted up the stairs toward her daughter's bedroom.

She stopped at the top of the stairs, shocked at the broken furniture, the splintered glass on the floor. Her vision tunneled and she saw Emma lying in a bloody heap at the end of the hallway. A man stood over her, a knife in his hand.

For a few seconds, Abigail was too stunned to move, her breath catching, throat closing. The man started toward her. Her eyes couldn't focus on any one thing. She went back and forth between the knife clenched in his bloody fist and her daughter's body on the floor.

'No—'

The man lunged toward her. Without thinking, Abigail stepped back. She tripped, falling down the stairs, hip and shoulder blades thumping the hard wood as she slid head first. There was a chorus of pain from her body: elbow hitting the stiles on the railing, anklebone cracking against the wall, a searing burn in her neck as she tried to keep her head from popping against the sharp tread of the stairs. She landed in the foyer, the breath knocked out of her lungs.

The dog. Where was the stupid dog?

Abigail rolled onto her back, wiping blood out of her eyes, feeling broken glass grind into her scalp.

The man was rushing down the stairs, the knife still in his hand. Abigail didn't think. She kicked up as he came off the last tread, lodging the toe of her sneaker somewhere between his asshole and his scrotum. She was far off the mark, but it didn't matter. The man stumbled, cursing as he went down on one knee.

She rolled onto her stomach and scrambled toward the door. He grabbed her leg, yanking her back so hard that a white-hot pain shot up her spine and into her shoulder. She clutched at the glass on the floor, trying to find a piece to hurt him with but the tiny shards only ripped open the skin of her hand. She started kicking at him, legs flailing wildly behind her as she inched toward the front door.

'Stop it!' he screamed, both his hands clamping down on her ankles. 'God dammit, I said stop!'

She stopped, trying to catch her breath, trying to think. Her head was still ringing, her mind unable to focus. Two feet ahead, the front door was still open, offering a view down the gentle slope of the walk to her car parked on the street. She twisted around so she could face her attacker. He still held her ankles to keep her from kicking. The knife was beside him on the floor.

His eyes were a sinister black – two pieces of granite showing beneath heavy lids. His broad chest rose and fell as he panted for breath. Blood soaked his shirt.

Emma's blood.

Abigail tensed her stomach muscles and lunged up toward him, fingers straight out as her nails stabbed into his eyes.

He slapped the side of her ear with his open palm but she kept at it, digging her thumbs into his eye sockets, feeling them start to give. His hands clamped around her wrists, forcing her fingers away. He was twenty times stronger than her, but Abigail was thinking of Emma now, that split second when she'd seen her daughter upstairs, the way her body was positioned, her shirt pushed up over her small breasts. She was barely recognizable, her head a bloody, red mass. He had taken everything, even her daughter's beautiful face.

'You bastard!' Abigail screamed, feeling like her arms were going to break as he pried her hands away from his eyes. She bit his fingers until teeth met with bone. The man screamed, but still held on. This time when Abigail brought up her knee, it made contact squarely between his legs.

The man's bloody eyes went wide and his mouth opened, releasing a huff of sour breath. His grip loosened but still did not release. As he fell onto his back, he pulled Abigail along with him.

Automatically, her hands wrapped around his thick neck. She could feel the cartilage in his throat move, the rings that lined the esophagus bending like soft plastic. His grip went tighter around her wrists but her elbows were locked now, her shoulders in line with her hands as she pressed all of her weight into the man's neck. Lightning bolts of pain shot through her shaking arms and shoulders. Her hands cramped as if thousands of tiny needles stabbed into her nerves. She could feel vibrations through her palms as he tried to speak. Her vision tunneled again. She saw starbursts of red dotting his eyes, his wet lips opening, tongue protruding. She was sitting on him, straddling him, and she became aware of the fact that she could feel the man's hipbones pressing into the meat of her thighs as he arched up, trying to buck her off.

Unbidden, she thought of Paul, the night they had made Emma – how Abigail had known, just known, that they were making a baby. She had straddled her husband like this, wanting to make sure she got every drop of him to make their perfect child.

And Emma *was* perfect . . . her sweet smile, her open face. The way she trusted everyone she met no matter how many times Paul warned her.

Emma lying upstairs. Dead. Blood pooled around her. Underwear yanked down. Her poor baby. What had she gone through? What humiliation had she suffered at the hands of this man?

Abigail felt a sudden warmness between her legs. The man had urinated on them both. He stared at her – really saw her – then his eyes glassed over. His arms fell to the side, hands popping against the glass-strewn tile. His body went limp, mouth gaping open.

Abigail sat back on her heels, looking at the lifeless man in front of her.

She had killed him.

Triptych

Karin Slaughter

Three people with something to hide. One killer with nothing to lose.

When Atlanta police detective Michael Ormewood is called out to a murder scene at the notorious Grady Homes, he finds himself faced with one of the most brutal killings of his career: Aleesha Monroe is found in the stairwell in a pool of her own blood, her body horribly mutilated.

As a one-off killing it's shocking, but when it becomes clear that it's just the latest in a series of similar attacks, the Georgia Bureau of Investigation are called in, and Michael is forced into working with Special Agent Will Trent of the Criminal Apprehension Team – a man he instinctively dislikes.

Twenty-four hours later, the violence Michael sees around him every day explodes in his own back yard. And it seems the mystery behind Monroe's death is inextricably entangled with a past that refuses to stay buried . . .

'This is without doubt an accomplished, compelling and complex tale, with page-turning power aplenty' *Daily Express*

'Criminally spectacular' *OK!*

arrow books

Skin Privilege
Karin Slaughter

It's no simple case of murder.

Lena Adams has spent her life struggling to forget her childhood in Reece, the small town which nearly destroyed her. She's made a new life for herself as a police detective in Heartsdale, a hundred miles away – but nothing could prepare her for the violence which explodes when she is forced to return. A vicious murder leaves a young woman incinerated beyond recognition. And Lena is the only suspect.

When Heartsdale police chief Jeffrey Tolliver, Lena's boss, receives word that his detective has been arrested, he has no choice but to go to Lena's aid – taking with him his wife, medical examiner Sara Linton. But soon after their arrival, a second victim is found. The town closes ranks. And both Jeffrey and Sara find themselves entangled in a horrifying underground world of bigotry and rage – a violent world which shocks even them. But can they discover the truth before the killer strikes again?

'No one does American small-town evil more chillingly . . . Slaughter tells a dark story that grips and doesn't let go'
The Times

'Thoroughly gripping' *Daily Mirror*

'Beautifully paced, appropriately grisly, and terrifyingly plausible' *Time Out*

arrow books

Faithless

Karin Slaughter

There are many ways to die. But some are more terrifying than others . . .

A walk in the woods takes a sinister turn for police chief Jeffrey Tolliver and medical examiner Sara Linton when they stumble across the body of a young girl. Incarcerated in the ground, all the initial evidence indicates that she has, quite literally, been scared to death.

But as Sara embarks on the autopsy, something even more horrifying comes to light. Something which shocks even Sara. Detective Lena Adams, talented but increasingly troubled, is called in from vacation to help with the investigation – and the trail soon leads to a neighbouring county, an isolated community and a terrible secret . . .

'Brutal and chilling' *Daily Mirror*

'*Faithless* confirms her at the summit of the school of writers specialising in forensic medicine and terror' *The Times*

arrow books

Indelible

Karin Slaughter

Some crimes can never be forgotten . . .

When medical examiner Sara Linton and police chief Jeffrey Tolliver take a trip away from the small town of Heartsdale, it should be a straightforward weekend at the beach. But they decide to take a detour via Jeffrey's hometown and things go violently wrong when Jeffrey's best friend Robert shoots dead an intruder who breaks into his home. Jeffrey and Sara are first on the scene and Jeffrey's keen to clear his friend's name, but for Sara things aren't so simple. And when Jeffrey appears to change the crime scene, Sara no longer knows who to trust.

Twelve years later, Sara and Jeffrey are caught up in a shockingly brutal attack which threatens to destroy both their lives. But they're not random victims. They've been targeted. And it seems the past is catching up with both of them . . .

'*Indelible* is a salutary reminder that Slaughter is one of the most riveting writers in the field today'
Sunday Express

'Brilliantly chilling'
heat

arrow books